"What the hell are you doing in my house?"

"Your house?" Clancey managed to croak. "This is my house!"

"Not anymore, it's not."

"I have the lease to prove it," she said, taking a single unwilling step backward.

That made him pause, but then he shook his head. "Your lease is no good, Miss—whatever your name is."

She ignored the half question. "It's perfectly in order. My landlord—"

"Your so-called landlord hasn't paid his property taxes in years. I paid them. Now I own the house." His voice took on a dry note. "So can I have an answer to my original question? What the hell are you doing in my house?"

"I'm going to run a toy store here."

"Oh, no, you're not," he said, looking appalled. "You'll have to get out."

Leigh Michaels started her fiction-writing career when she was in elementary school, by making up new endings to favorite books in order to put herself to sleep at night. And though those experiments in story-writing were never committed to paper, she says plotting them out was good practice for writing romance novels.

She has also written newspaper features, magazine articles, a textbook, short stories, poems, and—she estimates—two tons of letters. She likes hearing from readers. Write to her at P.O. Box 935, Ottumwa, Iowa, 52501-0935.

Books by Leigh Michaels

HARLEQUIN ROMANCE
3086—AN IMPERFECT LOVE
3119—AN UNCOMMON AFFAIR
3141—PROMISE ME TOMORROW
3171—GARRETT'S BACK IN TOWN
3184—OLD SCHOOL TIES
3214—THE BEST-MADE PLANS

HARLEQUIN PRESENTS
1107—CLOSE COLLABORATION
1147—A NEW DESIRE
1245—ONCE AND FOR ALWAYS
1266—WITH NO RESERVATIONS

Don't miss any of our special offers. Write to us at the following address for information on our newest releases.

Harlequin Reader Service
P.O. Box 1397, Buffalo, NY 14240
Canadian address: P.O. Box 603,
Fort Erie, Ont. L2A 5X3

THE UNEXPECTED LANDLORD
Leigh Michaels

Harlequin Books

TORONTO • NEW YORK • LONDON
AMSTERDAM • PARIS • SYDNEY • HAMBURG
STOCKHOLM • ATHENS • TOKYO • MILAN
MADRID • WARSAW • BUDAPEST • AUCKLAND

ISBN 0-373-03233-1

Harlequin Romance first edition November 1992

THE UNEXPECTED LANDLORD

Printed in U.S.A.

CHAPTER ONE

IF A CASUAL OBSERVER had wandered down Pine Street, climbed the steps to the old railed porch of the faded, mustard yellow house and come inside, the front room would have looked as if a dozen four-year-olds had spent the afternoon at play.

A tea set was jumbled on a small table by the wide front windows, and the matching chairs were overturned as if the party had been interrupted in midsip. A hundred teddy bears had cascaded over the area rug in front of the fireplace, and a group of racing cars lay upside down in a corner as if they had hit the wall at top speed. A pair of rocking horses stood awkwardly in a corner, nose to tail as if fending off flies in the wild.

But there was not even pretend tea in the tiny china cups. The teddy bears were too uncrushed ever to have known the hug of a child. The racing cars were still bright with paint, and the rocking horses proudly displayed every single strand of yarn in mane and tail.

And the casual observer couldn't come in, anyway—not until the weekend, when the sign would be hung on the porch rail and Small World would officially open in its new location.

Thank heaven for that much, Clancey Kincade thought. She still had two more full days before Friday's grand opening to reduce this mess to neatness, to make the place look like a toy store and not a warehouse that had been hit by an earthquake. And it was going to take every minute. The hallway was still stacked with boxes, the stockroom was piled, and as for the apartment upstairs—well, she'd spent last night on the living-room floor because she couldn't find all the pieces of her bed, and it looked as if tonight would be no different.

She took the last picture book from the box and placed it neatly on the lowest shelf next to the fireplace. Then, tucking a loose lock of strawberry blond hair back into her barrette, she pulled another box toward her. "I hope you don't mind working late, Eileen," she said. "I seem to have underestimated the amount of time it would take to get the other store closed and all the inventory moved and arranged."

A dark-haired young woman turned from the baby dolls she was arranging in a big antique cradle. "No, I don't mind. I've got nothing better to do, anyway. I'm certainly off parties at the moment, after that disaster last night."

"Why? Weren't there any eligible men?" Perhaps listening to the ongoing saga of Eileen's love life would take her mind off the cramp developing in her lower back. Sitting cross-legged on a hardwood floor was the only way to get these shelves arranged, so there was no point in complaining.

"Eligible? There was no one who was even interesting. The only man who was even a possibility turned out to be wearing a toupee." Eileen finished the cradle and began setting up collectors' dolls in a glass display case. "Is it asking too much for there to be one man in the world who's really my type?" she asked mournfully. "All it takes is *one.*"

Clancey tried to hide a smile. "You're beginning to sound desperate."

"Well, what if I am? I'm almost thirty."

"And your biological clock is starting to tick?"

"Don't laugh. When yours starts, you won't think it's a joke anymore. And face it, Clancey—when you're not drowning in work, you spend some time thinking about getting married, too."

"Oh? How do you know?"

"It's obvious. A woman doesn't start a toy store unless she's fond of kids. Besides, you wouldn't let Hank Gleason hang around if you weren't thinking of marrying him."

Clancey frowned. "What's wrong with Hank?"

"Frankly, watching ice melt would be more interesting."

Clancey unpacked two more boxes while she thought that one over. Eileen had a point; Hank was all right, but he didn't rate when it came to sheer excitement. "Hank isn't any more interested in a serious relationship than I am. He's too busy."

"So why do you keep going out with him?"

"Well, you don't meet eligible men by hanging around home. Besides, Hank and I have an arrangement. Neither of us has time to get involved right now, so seeing each other lets us have the occasional night out, and it keeps all our well-meaning friends from fixing us up with blind dates."

"If that was a warning, don't worry. If I find an eligible man, I certainly won't be fixing him up with my friends."

They worked for another hour in companionable silence, the only noises the rumble of traffic on Pine Street, the rustling of tissue paper and delicate fabrics, the ripping of tape and corrugated cardboard. The sun dropped low into the west, and the slanting late-afternoon light poured through the beveled-glass panel on the stair landing. Rainbows began to chase each other through the hallway.

Clancey finished the books, stretched gratefully and moved over to the pile of teddy bears. Each had a discreet loop sewed into the back of the neck, and she began to hang them one by one on a specially modified coat tree, turning it into a mountain of stuffed animals.

She saved her favorite for the very top. It was a panda bear, smaller than most of the others. It was the perfect size to share a baby's crib, in fact, and with more expression in his eyes than any other stuffed bear she'd ever seen. He looked a bit sad, actually, as if wondering how long he was going to have to wait to meet that special baby.

Clancey found herself cuddling the bear as if he were the infant in question. Maybe she should just take him upstairs for her own collection. Someday...

Darn Eileen and her biological clock, she thought. *Now she's got me started!*

She hastily put the bear into his place at the top of the coat tree and told herself not to be silly. It wasn't an urgent matter, after all. She was twenty-seven; she had plenty of time.

Eileen was around the corner in what had once been the dining room, arranging music boxes on the built-in sideboard. She was winding each one and letting it play, making certain the movement had survived the cross-town trip, and the resulting mosaic of lullabies was enough to drive sensitive ears mad.

"You're going about this all wrong, you know," Clancey said finally.

"What do you mean, wrong? You can't even see what I'm doing!"

Clancey peered into the room. "The music boxes? No, they're fine. I mean the way you've been looking for men."

Eileen leaned against the sideboard and fanned herself with her hand. "And I suppose you're the expert? What's wrong with my methods?"

"Well, they don't seem to be working, do they? Tell me again about the man with the toupee, for instance."

"What's to tell? That says it all, don't you think? I mean, a man who wears a *rug*, for heaven's sake—"

"He might be a wonderful man underneath the toupee. And he could take it off, you know. That last nut you dated had some faults that couldn't be removed so easily."

Eileen shrugged. "You never know unless you try. Some character defects just don't show up till you get better acquainted. He was certainly good-looking."

"That's part of the problem, you know. There's a limited number of rich and sexy guys out there, and—"

"I can't wait to hear your strategy for finding them," Eileen said sweetly. "There are such hordes of eligible men waiting on your doorstep. I think you're too weak from hunger to be logical, dear."

Clancey grinned. "You're right about that much. Why don't you run out for pizza? We can use a break."

"What you really mean is you need to finish thinking out this wonderful idea. Pepperoni, olives and extra cheese?" Eileen grabbed her jacket and purse and was already at the front door when Clancey nodded her agreement. She tugged on the handle. "Damn, the door's stuck again."

"That's because it's not the door that belongs here."

"It's because you forgot to call the locksmith."

Clancey planted a foot on the jamb and wrapped both hands around the knob. "That, too. I wonder what the original door looked like. It was probably very ornate, with beveled-glass sidelights to match the window upstairs—it's too big an opening for an ordinary door. And it would have been solid, so it wouldn't have warped like this modern monstrosity." The door relented with a screech. "There," she said, dusting her hands. "Just leave it slightly ajar till you get back."

"I could pick up a battering ram if you like," Eileen offered. "It might come in handy."

Clancey made a mental note—it was at least the hundredth item on her list—to call the locksmith first thing tomorrow, and washed her hands in the half-bath tucked beneath the front stairway. It was too tiny to be practical, and every time she looked at it she shuddered. The plumbing had been run through holes cut in the staircase, ruining the paneling.

Not that this house had ever been a mansion, exactly, she reminded herself. It wasn't big enough or grand enough for that. Even its location at the edge of the retail district indicated that its original owner had been only modestly wealthy. But it had once been a family's pride, that was obvious. It had been a gracious home with big rooms and pleasant views, with a floor plan that showed great thought. Now, after decades as an apartment house and a couple of years of standing empty, it showed the sad, tired signs of neglect and abuse.

She leaned against one of the twin pillars that supported the arched doorway between the entrance hall and the front parlor. At least, she thought, once upon a time the room had been a beautifully proportioned Victorian parlor. But that had been years ago, before the deep crown moldings had been covered with mud-colored paint, and before the corner had been knocked off the intricately carved mantel. She could see the grain of golden oak lurking under the layers of paint, and she longed to start sloshing paint remover around until the wood shone through again.

First things first, she told herself. Someday perhaps she would be able to do that, but not just yet. If all went well, and her move into this bigger space created the increase in profits she hoped for, she'd buy the house and start slowly renovating it, wiping out those marks of fatigue and neglect and abuse. In the meantime, the owner had agreed to a three-year lease, and that would let her get her feet on the ground, recuperate from the financial strain of the move, and be absolutely certain that this was the best permanent location for her business.

Footsteps sounded on the porch. Eileen must have found a pizza place nearby, she thought idly. That knowledge would be useful, with the busy retail season coming up. She'd have to work hard and put in long hours, but if she had a good Christmas season, she'd be well on her way to success.

She was straightening out the rocking horses so they stood primly side by side when the front door squealed open. "Well, that was certainly fast," she said over her shoulder. "I hope you got napkins and things, because I wouldn't be able to find any upstairs if I looked for a week."

There was no cheerful answer, no footsteps—just a deep, disquieting silence.

Clancey's skin started to quiver as if the individual cells were trying to run for cover. *The wind blew the door open,* she told herself.

But there was no wind. And in any case, even if a breeze was strong enough to open that heavy door, how could it turn around and close it? For the door *had* closed. There was no draft, no sensation of crisp fall air moving through the house. It was strictly an internal chill that was making Clancey's blood turn to ice.

Behind her, a masculine voice said, "What in the hell is going on here?"

She drew a shuddery breath, wishing she'd been less adamant on the subject of violent toys; even a plastic handgun would be a comfort just now—if it looked realistic.

She turned around slowly. Should she make a dash for the door or would it be better to try to get a good look so she could identify this intruder? If it was money he wanted, there was little enough of that here.

The question of getting a good look was a moot one; the figure was no more than a shadow in the hallway. The afternoon had faded so gradually into evening that Clancey hadn't even realized how dark it had become. All she could see was a general shape. He wasn't awfully tall, but that wasn't a lot of comfort since she was hardly an Amazon herself. He might not be huge, but he was a good six inches taller than she was, and he looked solidly built. He was wearing a soft cap with a narrow brim that shaded his face, and under his topcoat she could see the gleam of a white shirt, a striped tie and the edge of a jacket lapel—

A burglar who wears a suit to work? she thought. *This is incredible!*

This time his voice was a little louder. "I said, what the hell are you doing in my house? And what is all this—stuff?"

It wasn't an unpleasant voice; despite the tough-guy edge, it had a mellow sort of undertone that made Clancey think of soft summer days. Then she realized what he'd said.

"Your house?" she managed to croak. "This is my house!"

He wasn't a burglar, then. Just an ordinary run-of-the-mill psycho, confused about the facts. Or perhaps he was drunk and had simply stumbled into the wrong house.

Some comfort that is, Clancey, she told herself dryly.

The shadowed figure went on. "Not anymore, it's not. I assume that you're Leonard Schultz's—what? Not wife, surely."

She wasn't quite sure whether he had intended to insult her, but it certainly felt that way. "You got that much right," she snapped. "And I'm not his daughter, either." Reluctantly she had to admit that he didn't have the wrong house, or he wouldn't know the owner's name. And he didn't sound mentally off balance. Or drunk. But if he was sober and in his right mind, what on earth was going on?

"Lady friend, then?" He didn't sound interested. "You don't look quite the type, but . . ."

Now she was certain she should feel offended. "Thank you very much for that observation!"

"My pleasure. In any case, it doesn't matter what good old Leonard is to you." Slowly he started to move toward her.

Clancey took a single, unwilling step back. "He's my landlord," she said hastily. Her voice trembled a little, despite her best efforts to keep it steady.

"He can't be."

"He is so. I have a lease to prove it."

That made him pause for an instant, but then he shook his head and took another step toward her. "It doesn't matter what you have, because he doesn't own the place anymore. I do."

There was such a note of certainty in his voice that it was impossible not to believe him.

Clancey gasped. "Do you mean to tell me he sold it? That sleazy crumb-cake! He didn't even let me know! When?"

His words came slowly and deliberately. "I got full possession just today, but—"

Relief washed over her in a wave. "Today? Well, then it doesn't matter. You'll have to take it up with Leonard—I mean the little matter of not telling you about a tenant when he signed the papers."

"Your lease is no good, Miss—whatever your name is."

She ignored the half question. "It's perfectly in order. My lawyer approved it. And since I signed it six weeks ago, I'm sure it predates the sale."

But was it possible that good old Leonard had already sold the property before he wrote the lease? He wasn't known around the city as the most ethical of businessmen, but surely he wouldn't pull a stunt as clearly illegal as that, would he? And even if he'd tried, Hank would have caught it when he looked over the lease and checked out the details.

"It's a matter of common sense," she went on, "that existing leases take priority. I'm sure you'll find that in your sales contract somewhere. It's a standard clause, I believe. So accept my congratulations on your purchase, and I'll see you in three years when my lease is up and it's time to renegotiate. Good night.''

She took a step toward him and put a hand on his arm to urge him to the door. Under the buttery-soft tweed sleeve of his coat, his arm was warm and solid.

Very solid, Clancey thought. *Immovable, in fact. So now what do I do?*

She backed away again. He didn't seem to notice he'd been touched at all.

''There is no sales contract,'' he said, ''so leases don't come into it. I didn't exactly buy the house in the usual way.''

Clancey took a deep breath, held it, and counted to ten. It wasn't far enough, but it helped a little. ''If you're going to tell me that you won it from him playing poker—''

He shook his head. ''In a tax sale.''

''What?'' she said faintly.

''Your precious so-called landlord hasn't paid his property taxes for years. I paid them, so now I own the house. The details don't matter. However, since Leonard doesn't own it anymore—'' his voice took on a dry note as he quoted her own words back to her ''—it's a matter of common sense that he can't lease it to anyone.''

Ever so slowly, he'd been advancing on her. Clancey had been backing away, just as slowly. Now she bumped into the dollhouse at the end of the parlor, hard enough that some of the tiny furniture toppled. The delicate chandeliers swung and rattled from the shock of the collision. They sounded the way her nerves felt.

"Now that I've explained myself," he added patiently, "can I have an answer to my original question? What the hell are you doing in my house?"

Her voice had gone flat and lifeless. "I am going to run a toy store here."

"No, you're not. You'll have to get out."

"I will not! You haven't shown me any evidence to convince me you're telling the truth. You've just burst in here with an incredible story and you expect me to pack up everything I own and leave on your unsupported word? Forget it."

"Mark my ungentlemanly conduct down to the shock of finding you in what's supposed to be an empty house."

He didn't sound like a gentleman, she thought. "I don't even know who you are. Maybe you're a psychotic personality after all, with some kind of grudge against Leonard."

He smiled. At least, she thought it was a smile, but it didn't last long enough for her to be certain. "It's not hard to imagine all kinds of people having a grudge against Leonard," he conceded. "And they wouldn't necessarily be psychotic, either. Let me see this lease of yours."

Clancey put her chin up. "Show me proof that you own the house. I'm betting you don't even have a key—explain that one, if you can. If I hadn't left the door open, you probably couldn't have gotten in at all."

"I'd have knocked out a window," he countered. "It's not breaking and entering when you're locked out of your own house, you know, and owners don't generally hand over things like keys and blueprints and instructions on the balky water heater when they've lost the property in a tax sale."

She had to admit the truth of that, but she wasn't going to give up her advantage. "Perhaps. But it's a pretty flaky story."

"Tomorrow morning I will be back with not only the deed, but the legal papers to evict you. So you'd better take my advice, and be packed and ready to go." He touched the brim of his cap in a gesture that parodied a respectful salute.

She clutched the edge of the dollhouse table so hard her fingers ached.

Just as he reached the pillars, the front door creaked open and the lights in the hall flashed on. "What's with the dark, Clancey?" Eileen called. "You can't get anything done in the—" She broke off awkwardly as she saw the visitor.

He tipped his hat to her and left without a word.

Eileen swallowed hard and watched him out of sight. Then she came across the room toward Clancey, the pizza box balanced like a waiter's tray on one upraised hand. "I take it all back," she said confidingly. "If your system of manhunting can produce results like that, I think I'll give it a try after all. Have a piece of pizza and tell me how to do it."

IN LESS THAN FIFTEEN minutes he had destroyed what Clancey had worked five years to gain. That was the fact of it, in one tiny blunt package. Five years of struggle, first to gather enough seed money to convince the bank to lend her the necessary capital, and then to build her business and her client base until she could point to Small World with pride.

And now it was all going down the drain.

If she couldn't open the store on schedule, Clancey didn't know what she would do. She couldn't possibly find another place on such short notice and get it ready. It would be difficult enough to find adequate warehouse space to store her inventory while she sought out another location. And every day that went by would make it more difficult—sales would be lost and regular clients would seek out other stores. They might never come back to her, even if she got on her feet again. And it was already October. Christmas was around the corner. She'd not only miss out on her most profitable sales period, but she'd have to dig deep into her capital to pay for storage space. She didn't have cash to fall back on, because she had sunk most of her money into advertising her new location. And suddenly she was without a place to live, as well.

Don't panic, she told herself. *You're assuming that he was telling the truth. You're assuming that he's right about everything he said. But it's just as likely that* you're *right. You've got a lease....*

And an attorney. Hank Gleason might not be her first choice for a passionate lover, but he was a more than adequate lawyer. Hank could tell her what her rights were where this—person—was involved. He would listen to her story, and then he'd check up on this—person. Whoever he was.

She groaned. That wasn't going to make Hank's job any easier, not even knowing who he was dealing with.

Damn, why hadn't she had the brains to at least ask the man's name? Why hadn't she insisted on getting a look at him? She could run headlong into him on the street and not even know him—unless her hand happened to rest on his arm. The solid feel of him she was sure she'd recognize. But as for his face...

Eileen would have been helpful on that question, Clancey was positive. She'd certainly gotten a good look at him, in the glare of the hallway lights. But Clancey wasn't sure she could bear to listen to Eileen on the subject, so she sent her home, phoned Hank and promptly embarrassed both of them by bursting into tears.

She managed to blubber through her story, but it didn't get easier, especially as Hank sounded increasingly grim with every word he spoke. "I'll do the best I can, Clancey, but it's going to take time to track down how all this happened. And you know I can't even start to check on it till morning when the courthouse opens."

Clancey felt her last bit of hope slide away. In the morning Hank would start to work. But the morning was also when he—that nameless "he," again!—had promised to come back with eviction orders and throw her out. And she had no doubt he would do his best to keep that promise.

Time. Hank needed time to figure out a strategy.

And time was the one thing Clancey didn't have.

CHAPTER TWO

CLANCEY WAS UP EARLY, sitting morosely in the window seat at the front of the house, drinking coffee just to keep herself busy, and hoping that something would delay the inevitable long enough for Hank to bring matters to a screeching halt. Surely he could find grounds to stop this. It was so bloody unfair.

But what was it Hank had told her last night? Something about a great many things being unfair but still perfectly legal. Not much of a comfort to feel that your own attorney had somehow ended up on the other side.

It was barely eight o'clock when a car pulled into the driveway and her annoying visitor of last night started up the front walk.

He was alone. There would be no sheriff's deputies, then, to serve papers and drag her belongings out into the street. That was some relief. Or perhaps it only meant they were coming along later, in case she balked.

"I could pretend not to be here," she muttered. "If I simply don't answer the door, what can he do? Break it down?"

Yes, she remembered. He had threatened last night to break in a window. He wouldn't hesitate.

So when the first firm knock sounded on the massive front door, she dragged herself up from the window seat and went to open it. She found herself hoping the door would jam so completely there would be no question of getting it open. Then he would have to stand outside and yell his demands. Like all inanimate objects, however, the door seemed to know precisely how to be most annoying at any given moment. It opened smoothly and sweetly and silently at the merest touch, and for the first time Clancey saw the face of the stranger who was ruining her life.

He was younger than she'd expected. It surprised her to realize that he couldn't be much over thirty. It might have been the conservative topcoat and the soft cap he'd been wearing the night before that had made her assess him differently, but on this sunny fall morning he was wearing neither. He wasn't casually dressed, however; his navy blazer and gray trousers were obviously the garb of some sort of professional man, and the pin-striped shirt and muted tie finished off the picture in perfectly coordinated fashion.

He was on his way to work, she told herself, and he had just stopped by for a minute to deal with a minor nuisance before he got down to the day's important business. The suspicion that this problem, catastrophic as it was to her, might be classified in his mind with a dozen other petty ones infuriated her, and she had an unreasonable impulse to grab a handful of his hair and tug. He had dark hair, so close to black that it had a bluish sheen, and he wore it a little longer than she had thought last night—it wouldn't be hard to get a good enough grip on it to gain his attention, that was sure.

"Sorry about the hammering," he said. "The doorbell seems to be broken."

She wasn't in a mood to play games. "Complain to the owner," she snapped. "I only rent the place."

He actually looked a little apologetic. His eyes—they were deep set and dark blue, with almost a hint of sea green in the depths—met hers in earnest appraisal but no animosity. It was almost as if he was silently pleading with her to be reasonable.

That's foolish, she told herself. *There's no compromise for this problem.*

Clancey put her arm firmly across the doorway. "I believe you said you'd have some papers for me. Unless you do, I'm not letting you in."

His hand moved to the inside breast pocket of his jacket. "I have the deed but not the eviction papers," he admitted.

She tipped her head back and stared up at him, eyes narrowed. "Oh? What happened? Did you discover you couldn't throw me out so easily, after all?"

"No." His voice was level. "I thought perhaps after our conversation last night you'd have accepted the inevitable and gone away. I see I was daydreaming."

Behind her back, Clancey's fingers curled into a fist, and she had to remind herself that hitting him wouldn't help the situation. Her eyes dropped to the document in his hand. It certainly looked real enough.

"Since we are going to have to deal with each other," he said, "don't you think we should start with names, Miss—?"

There was no point in trying to continue to be anonymous. "Kincade," she said reluctantly. "Clancey Kincade."

There was a tiny span of silence. Clancey was used to it; there was inevitably a pause when she introduced herself, and it was always followed by the unavoidable question, *How on earth did you get a crazy name like that?*

But he didn't ask. She was almost disappointed.

He passed over the document, instead. "This isn't a copy, because I thought you'd insist on having the official deed in your hands. I might point out, however, that destroying it will not delay or change anything, merely send me back to the courthouse for a duplicate."

"I wouldn't think of destroying—" She glanced at the paper and said, without thinking, "How in the world did you get a name like—" She stopped herself by biting her tongue, hard. *Rowan McKenna.* It was unusual, there was no doubt about that. It certainly explained the fine-tuned, dark good looks; that was the Celtic strain in him.

He looked injured. "I would have thought any woman named Clancey would understand."

She suspected that the hurt was a sham, purely a tactic to manipulate her into embarrassed concessions, and she wasn't about to apologize. "I suppose you might as well come in, Mr. McKenna."

Once inside, he put the deed safely back in his pocket and asked politely, "May I see your lease?"

She passed it to him silently and stood drinking her cold coffee while he scanned it.

Finally he refolded the pages and slapped them casually against the palm of his hand a couple of times. He seemed to be staring at the teddy-bear tree, but Clancey wouldn't have bet that he was seeing anything at all.

Then he said very quietly, "Miss Kincade, I understand that this has been a terrible shock to you, and I don't want to be unreasonable. I'll give you a few days—shall we say a week?—to move out."

She blinked in astonishment. "That's quite a concession, coming from you. I can only conclude that my lease must look pretty solid."

"As leases go, yes, but that still doesn't make it valid. I don't have to make concessions. I'm giving you a little leeway out of the goodness of my heart. If you'd rather have it otherwise, I'll go downtown right now and get the eviction papers."

She was already regretting her rash words. He'd handed her a delay, a little time for Hank to dig around, and she'd practically thrown it back in his face! She said quickly, "No, it's very thoughtful of you. Look, would you like coffee?"

He eyed her cup. "Is it safe?"

"Of course," she said crisply. "I've never seen a need to keep cyanide in my kitchen. Until now."

The corner of his mouth twitched, but his voice was solemn. "I'd love a cup of coffee."

He followed her through the parlor and the adjoining dining room into the kitchen. Clancey dumped out the overbrewed contents of the coffeemaker and filled it with fresh grounds and cold water. As she turned, she caught him glancing up the twisting back stairway as if he was wondering what lay at the top of it now.

"I haven't hurt the place," she said defensively. "In fact, most of the walls have had a fresh coat of paint since I took possession. And all that work and cost isn't the only thing I stand to lose in this deal—there's the security deposit I paid Leonard Schultz, and the rent in advance, and—" Her shoulders began to sag.

I am not going to cry, she told herself fiercely. She swallowed hard and said, "I don't think you understand how important this is to me. My whole life is at stake here. My business is going to fail if you force me to move."

"How about just going back to wherever you came from? This isn't a new venture, is it? I'm sure I've seen the name somewhere before." He gestured toward the Small World sign propped against the overloaded table, its fresh paint bright with a promise that would now probably never come true.

Clancey moved the sign to the back porch, its face to the wall so she wouldn't have to look at it, and cleared a corner of the table. "No, Small World isn't new. But I certainly can't go back to where I came from. The storefront is already leased." She put a couple of mugs down on the table with more force than she'd intended.

He didn't respond. "Do you mind if I take my coat off?" he asked instead. "It's a bit warm in here, don't you think?"

"The boiler works wonderfully. I'm sure you'll find that news a comfort. After the doorbell and all—" Clancey's voice started to tremble. She turned her back and watched the coffeemaker as if it was likely to explode without supervision. By the time it finished the cycle she had herself under control again.

"Look," she said earnestly, pulling up a chair across from him. "You own the house now. You've got what you want, right? I'm actually a benefit, you know, if you'll just look at it that way. You won't have to advertise for a tenant for three whole years. And since I'm renting both apartments, you won't even have squabbles between your renters. You've got nothing to worry about. It's a great deal—"

"It might be," he interrupted, "if I wanted a tenant."

"Oh," Clancey said weakly. "You mean you were planning to use the space yourself?"

He said, "Why do people usually buy houses, Miss Kincade?"

"To live in? You want to renovate the place and move in?" She looked around as if she'd never seen the kitchen before. "It isn't going to be cheap."

"Don't you think that's my problem—not yours?"

"You could let me stay, and put all the rent money I pay into a fund, and then when you start work on the house..."

He shook his head.

Clancey sighed. "I suppose, with my luck, you're a banker or a stockbroker, or somebody else made of money."

"I'm a certified public accountant."

"Oh. That means you already have budgets and things lined up."

"And time schedules—which you, Miss Kincade, are interfering with. A week, I believe we said?" He didn't wait for an answer as he pushed his chair back. "I hope you don't mind if I look around a bit before I leave?"

Clancey shrugged. "Be my guest," she said, with a twinge of irony. She picked up the empty cups and started for the sink.

He glanced at the twisting stairs again. "Is this stairway blocked off at the top?"

"No, it's open, same as it was when—" Her eyes narrowed with curiosity. "You sound as if you've never seen the place."

"I haven't," he said calmly. "Not the inside."

"You actually bought a house you'd never seen?"

"Well, Leonard wasn't keen on the idea of giving tours to prospective owners." He vanished up the back stairs, leaving Clancey with her mouth ajar.

She could hear him walking through the rooms, picking his way among the piles of boxes and crates. Then for a while she heard nothing at all. Had he found the attic stairs, or was he inspecting her belongings?

She washed the cups and wandered back into the parlor. Since she had nothing better to do, she began to straighten up the dollhouse, putting back into place the furniture that had been knocked over when she collided with it. She was standing there with a six-inch-tall grandfather clock in her hand when Rowan McKenna came down the front stairs, whistling.

"Well, what do you think now?" she asked. "It needs an awful lot of work, doesn't it? Maybe you should give up on the renovation and just rent it out and recoup your investment as fast as you can."

He shook his head. "This is a great house." He actually patted her on the shoulder as he said it. "It's everything I hoped for, and then some. I've never seen a hexagonal stair landing before. Oh, the roof needs work, and the plumbing is awful, but that's no more than I expected. You'll be out in a week, right?"

Clancey's fingers clenched convulsively, crushing the grandfather clock. The sharp crack of splintering plastic was echoed by something smashing deep inside her, and she put her chin up. "No," she said hoarsely. "I won't. The truth is that giving me a week wouldn't be any better than throwing me out right now."

He was very still, as if he'd frozen into position. She was already starting to recognize that motionless waiting of his as something threatening, but she didn't care.

"I've got no place to go and no money to finance another move," she went on recklessly. "I'm finished if I can't stay here. My business will be dead if I lose the Christmas season, and I'll be bankrupt. So I'm not moving at all, Mr. McKenna. Go ahead—just try to throw me out."

He shrugged. "If that's the way you want it."

"And in the meantime I'll be doing a little legal work of my own."

"Personally, I'd suggest you sue Leonard Schultz."

"Oh, don't worry, I will. And I'll sue you for being in collusion with him. And I'll sue the county, the city, the school board—everybody that collects taxes on this property—"

"You can't do that."

"How much would you like to bet on it? There's a thing called—" She groped through her memory for something Hank had said last night. "Due process, that's what it's called. They can't take something away from a citizen without notification, and I wasn't notified."

"Dammit, you weren't here then!"

She squared her shoulders. "Maybe I wasn't, but I've certainly been here for most of the past six weeks, painting and cleaning and putting up shelves. Don't you think it looks a little strange that nobody noticed me? Didn't you ever drive by your precious house, Mr. McKenna, and dream of when it would really be yours? A judge might wonder why you supposedly never saw lights or activity!" She seized the nearest box, heedless of the contents, and ripped off the sealing tape with her fingernails.

"You'll lose."

"Then I'll appeal. Who knows? It might take a year or two—or even three—to get it all straightened out in the courts. In the meantime, I'm having a grand opening this weekend. So I'm going to go right on unpacking." With a defiant gesture she dumped the box out at his feet. Hundreds of watercolor markers in a rainbow of shades rattled across the hardwood floor.

Rowan McKenna watched them roll. Only when the last one had come to rest at the far end of the dining room, and silence had once more descended on Small World, did he say, "I'll see you later, Miss Kincade."

The moment he was gone Clancey sat down with a bang among the markers. She pushed them away with a violent thrust of her arm and stretched out full-length, her head buried in her arms, her body racked with sobs.

She'd never felt so helpless in her life.

SHE WAS WAITING FOR HANK when he came into the restaurant precisely at one o'clock. He stooped to put a whisper of a kiss on her cheek and said, "I don't have much time, so we need to get our order in right away." After the waitress left he pulled out his chair and looked across at Clancey. "Just tea and toast? Is that all you want?"

"I haven't got any appetite."

"Wish that would happen to me when I get stressed out." He studied her. "You look awful, you know."

"Just awful? That's a relief." He didn't look great himself today, Clancey thought. He seemed tired, and the collar of his white shirt was a little too tight, as if he'd gained weight again.

Hank unwrapped a cracker and munched it. "So far I haven't found out much. Has the sheriff served papers on you?"

"No. I don't think Mr. McKenna has even filed a complaint yet. He seemed to be relying on logic and charm to convince me."

Hank stopped chewing. "Which McKenna?"

"Rowan. Why? Do you know him?"

His long exhalation was answer enough. "And he tried charm? I didn't know he had any."

Even in the midst of her despair, Clancey couldn't help wishing Eileen had been there to hear that one. The idea of Hank Gleason commenting on Rowan McKenna's lack of charm had a certain subtle irony that Eileen would have appreciated.

"Well, it didn't work," she pointed out. "I ended up threatening to sue him and everybody else who ever touched the paperwork on that house, and—"

Hank was shaking his head. "Oh, Clancey." The waitress set a chef's salad in front of him, and he drenched it in blue cheese dressing and dug in. "Clancey, honey."

Clancey eyed her whole-wheat toast without enthusiasm. "Well, I *can* sue him, can't I?"

"You could file suit against the man in the moon, too, but it doesn't mean you'd get anywhere."

"But it all takes time," she argued. "Hank, how could this happen, anyway?"

"It's a long process, set up with all sorts of delays just so this kind of thing can't happen."

"What a comfort!"

"There are waiting periods on top of waiting periods, but the only one that concerns us is the last ninety days. That's when the papers are filed by the new owner declaring his intention to take the place over. The house is inspected, and final notices are sent out to the owner, who has one last chance to redeem the property. At the same time, anybody else with an interest in the property is notified, so they can protect themselves."

"Like tenants?" Clancey asked.

"Exactly. Except in this case the house was empty when the notice was filed, and everybody assumed it would stay that way."

"How can that be legal?"

"Well, it wasn't unreasonable, Clancey. It's been empty for two years. That one careless assumption is just about the only thing we've got on our side if we try to sue McKenna—and he wasn't even the one who did the assuming. It doesn't look promising."

"I don't care," she said stubbornly. "I can try to make his life as miserable as he's making mine."

"On the other hand, you've got a great case against Leonard Schultz for misrepresentation."

"What's the point of suing him?" Clancey asked. "If Leonard had any money, he'd have paid his taxes."

"Not necessarily, but I'll check on his financial condition. It's still the best chance we've got."

"But that won't help me right now."

"No, I'm afraid it won't."

"So we've got to sue McKenna to slow things down."

He sighed. "All right, if you want to pursue it, I'll draw up the paperwork for an injunction to keep him from throwing you out, and then we'll go from there."

"You can do that? So he actually can't evict me?"

"I'll try," he warned. "I'm not guaranteeing the judge will go along with it."

Clancey shrugged. ''It's better than nothing. When will I know? At the moment I haven't any idea whether I should be getting ready for the grand opening or starting to pack up everything I own again.''

''I'll get the papers drawn as soon as I can.''

''That's great.'' Impulsively she reached across the table to give his hand a quick squeeze. ''I don't know what I'd do without you, Hank.''

He grinned. ''You finally noticed that?'' But he was looking at his watch even as he said it.

When Clancey got back to Pine Street everything looked just as usual. There wasn't a pyramid of toys in the center of the street, and there were no padlocks on the door. Clancey stopped on the sidewalk to gaze up at the house.

How dare it look so innocent, she wondered. It shouldn't be standing there in the fall sunshine like any ordinary old house; it ought to have a storm cloud crouched over it, at least.

But it looked just as charming as it had on the first day she'd seen it, in midsummer when she'd been enjoying the semiannual walking tour through the nearby historical restoration district. The house had delighted her with its jumbled mix of architectural features—the dormer windows in the attic that weren't quite symmetrically aligned, and the hexagonal protrusion on the lower floors that looked as if the builder had intended to construct a tower but changed his mind halfway through the job. The chipped and faded mustard yellow paint had been a soft splash of color against the glossy green and blue of a summer day. Now it formed a muted background for the brilliant orange foliage of the huge sugar maple at the corner of the porch and the long row of bright red burning bushes that marked the property line.

It had all looked so simple, back in July when she started to think about moving and expanding Small World.

"But that's what you get for falling in love before you check out the facts," Clancey muttered with a sigh.

Inside, Eileen was curled up in the rocking chair beside the fireplace reading *Anne of Green Gables*. "I needed something to keep me occupied," she said. "It was driving me nuts to look at this mess and not know what to do with it."

"Unpack."

Eileen jumped up. "Really? Hank's sure we can stay?"

Not exactly, Clancey thought, but it couldn't hurt to have faith, could it?

Having her hands busy helped relieve her worry a little, and the afternoon hours went by quickly. The adrenaline rush they both seemed to be experiencing helped them to make a bigger dent in the mess than Clancey would have expected, and by the end of the day the whole place looked almost organized.

She was setting up the cash register at the foot of the front stairs and trying to figure out a way to get more light right where she needed it when she heard a knock. It was beginning to sound familiar.

This time the door jammed. Rowan McKenna put his shoulder to it just as Clancey tugged, and she almost went sprawling. "Damn door," she muttered as he came in.

"Does it do that regularly?"

"Often enough," she admitted.

"How were you planning to get customers in and out?"

For an instant hope flared in her heart, and then she realized his phrasing was strictly past tense.

"Don't fret, I wasn't going to complain to you about it." She eyed him thoughtfully. He'd changed clothes since his morning visit. He was wearing casual trousers and a royal blue sweater over a pastel shirt. The cap was back, tilted rakishly to the side, and he had one hand in the pocket of a lightweight leather jacket.

She felt rather grubby all of a sudden in her faded jeans and sweatshirt. But who wanted to impress Rowan McKenna, anyway?

He brought his other hand out from behind his back, and she realized he was carrying a paper bag from a fast-food place.

"Planning to stay awhile?" she asked coolly.

"However long it takes. But this isn't my dinner—it occurred to me that it's my turn to provide the coffee." He took two paper cups out of the bag and popped the lids off.

The sheer reasonableness of the gesture alarmed her. She plugged in the cash register and started to arrange supplies in the cabinet below. Her hands were trembling.

She knew she should wait and see what he had to say, but she was afraid if she once let him start, she'd never be able to counter his arguments. On the other hand, the fact that he was here alone might indicate that Hank had been successful in getting the injunction....

"I've talked to my attorney," she said. "And we're going to do our best to tie things up as long as we can."

He didn't seem surprised. "Hank Gleason is known for that kind of legal action. It's about the only kind he's good at."

If he knew who her attorney was, he'd been checking things out. Or Hank had already filed the papers. "It's going to cost you a lot."

"I know," he said wryly. "I can add."

"Really? I'll bet that comes in handy with your job." But the flippant note was sheer bravado.

He sipped his coffee. "It will cost you plenty, too, if you fight."

That's funny, she thought. He sounds almost sorry about it.

She shrugged. "Only money. And if I don't fight— well, then it will cost me everything." She closed the cash drawer and looked up at him. "I don't have anything more to lose, you see, so I might as well go down fighting. I'll carry through with it. You can bet on that."

"I know. I recognize desperation when I see it."

Clancey's knees started to shake.

"So I've got a sort of deal to suggest."

His voice was almost gentle. *Almost,* she thought. Or was there actually a threat under the softness?

"How about it, Clancey Kincade?" he asked. "Do you want to talk, or not?"

CHAPTER THREE

CLANCEY STARED AT HIM. "Sure. What have I got to lose?" She tried to sound hard-boiled, as a good negotiator would, but it didn't quite work out that way. "What kind of a deal?"

The corner of his mouth twitched. "One we can both live with, I think. Why don't you get a jacket and come walk around the block with me?" She hesitated, and he added wryly, "Don't worry, if your murdered body turns up in a Dumpster somewhere, I'll be the first one they come looking for, and I know it."

"I'd still be just as dead," Clancey objected, but she got her windbreaker anyway. She made it a point, however, to tell Eileen where she was going.

When she turned back to Rowan McKenna, there was a thoughtful look in his face. "On the other hand," he speculated, "maybe I wouldn't be first on the list of suspects. If you have this abrasive effect on other people, it might be worth taking a chance...."

She ignored him. The evening air had cooled off in a hurry, and she shivered on the front steps as he stopped to zip up his jacket.

They walked halfway down the block before either broke the silence, but finally he said, "You've mentioned the Christmas season a couple of times. That's what you're really concerned about right now—correct?"

She rolled her eyes a little, but she answered as seriously as she could. "Of course. How successful would a toy store be if you took away Santa Claus? Nearly half my annual sales end up under someone's Christmas tree."

They rustled through a pile of leaves on the sidewalk. "It's only October," he mused.

It was obviously just the beginning of a line of argument, but Clancey cut it off short. "That's right, but I've already started my Christmas advertising campaign. And you don't move a retail business in the middle of the busiest season—even if you have somewhere to go." She wanted to add that all this was elementary business that any certified public accountant ought to have learned long before he took his board exams, but she decided there was no sense in insulting the man until she knew exactly what he was proposing.

"And after Christmas?" he prompted.

Clancey couldn't quite see where this was leading, but she couldn't deny the truth, either. "Sales drop off. It's the slowest time of year, in fact."

"So an interruption in business would be less disruptive."

"It would hurt less, yes," she conceded, and couldn't hold back any longer. "What kind of accountant are you, anyway, that you don't know all this stuff?"

"Making assumptions is what got us both into this situation," he pointed out. "Here's my proposal. You can stay through the Christmas season. Then you move—both you and the store—without further argument or delay."

Clancey dug her hands deep into the pockets of her jeans and bit her tongue to keep from agreeing instantly. It was far from ideal from her point of view. She'd have to face the grinding demands of the Christmas sales season with the need to find a new location for the store hanging over her head. But what alternative did she have? Compared to the present situation, it looked like manna from heaven.

"Why would you agree to that?" she asked suspiciously.

"Regardless of what you may think, I am not Simon Legree. Besides, I expect a promise in return—no more threats of frivolous lawsuits and no convoluted claims against me or my house. Ever."

"I see. You're afraid I'd win the case."

"No. I know perfectly well you'd lose—eventually—but we might as well save the costs of the battle. We both have better uses for the money than to give it to people like Gleason."

She glanced up at him through her lashes. "He doesn't waste any respect on you, either," she murmured.

"I'm not surprised. He wasn't very happy with the outcome the last time we disagreed."

Clancey concluded, regretfully, that there was no plausible excuse for asking for details. "I thought you were anxious to get the house."

"I am. I've waited a long time for this deal to come through." His voice was flat. "But another three months won't kill me, if I'm free and clear at the end of it."

She walked on. "This agreement only includes you, right?"

In the yellow glow of a streetlight she saw his eyebrows lift and draw together.

She added hastily, "I mean, I could still sue Leonard?"

"I hope you do," he said, teeth gritted. "He's the one who deserves it."

They turned the last corner and the house came back into view.

"All right," Clancey said. "It's a deal."

He nodded. "Then the place is yours till the first day of January, at the same terms as in your lease with Leonard."

"How about the first of February?" Clancey bargained. "You said I could stay the Christmas season, and there's such a thing as inventory reduction after the holiday, you know."

"The size of your inventory is not my problem. Price it right, and you won't have to worry about it."

"But—"

"Would you rather give up the house on the day after Christmas?" There was no mistaking the threat.

She smiled up at him. "January first," she conceded.

There was satisfaction in his tone. "I thought you might see sense."

They shook hands on it under the sugar maple at the corner of the house. Rowan McKenna's hand was strong and firm, and it was with reluctance that Clancey let her fingers slip out of that comfortable grip. She hadn't realized how cold she had become on that short walk. How had he managed to stay so warm?

She thrust her hands into the pockets of her jacket and hunched her shoulders against the crisp evening air. There didn't seem to be anything left to say, and yet he was still standing there as if he expected something more.

She looked over his shoulder at the house. Eileen had turned on the rest of the lights, and the glow spilled out of the windows and across the porch, casting long shadows on the frosty grass. Inside a warm and welcoming haven waited, ready to envelop the chilled and weary traveler.

She looked up at Rowan McKenna. He had turned a little in order to follow her gaze, and the beam of a street lamp fell across his face, accenting the chiseled lines of his profile and catching in the thick dark lashes to throw heavy shadows down across the strong cheekbones.

She could tell from his eyes that he was thinking the same thing she was—that the house was waiting for her. Not for him, not yet. His dream would have to wait.

Her heart twisted. It was no wonder that he was anxious to have his house, to realize the potential that was so apparent only at this hour of the night, when all the work waiting to be done faded into the soft shadows and the simple promise of loveliness remained.

"It's very generous of you," she said. There was a little catch in her voice; it was hardly more than a whisper. "Rowan—thank you for giving me a break."

He turned his head to look down at her, and smiled.

It was a long, slow smile that started with a sparkle in his blue-green eyes and lit his whole face. There were tiny laugh lines by his eyes, she saw, and his teeth gleamed white in the harsh light from the street lamp. The transformation startled her so much that she almost stopped breathing.

He touched two fingers to the brim of his cap and then he was gone, leaving her standing there in the cold air with her arms folded across her chest to conserve what warmth her body still possessed. *And Hank said Rowan McKenna didn't possess any kind of charm!*

HANK WASN'T PLEASED, when he stopped by Small World the next morning, to find that the work he'd done was in vain because the injunction was no longer needed.

"You could at least have called me as soon as you and McKenna worked out this little deal." His voice was level, but Clancey knew quite well that he was exerting icy control to keep it that way. "I ought to have been preparing for a client's tax hearing, but I interrupted that to take care of your emergency. Then to find out that it's no emergency at all..."

Clancey, who was kneeling on the floor to finish a model train layout, looked up and said contritely, "I'm sorry, Hank. I was so happy to have things worked out that I truly just forgot."

"That will not be a great comfort to my client. It's an important hearing. It could cost him millions."

"Well, everything's relative, isn't it?" Clancey muttered.

Eileen called from the hallway, "Look what I found hanging around outside, Clancey. I brought him in the back way rather than fight with the front door. Have you phoned the locksmith yet?"

Clancey didn't reply. She was watching Rowan, who'd followed Eileen across the hallway and was now leaning against the cash register table and looking at Hank with a wary gleam in his eyes.

Clancey scrambled up from the floor. "Did you come around to tell me where to pay the rent, and all that sort of detail?"

Rowan's dark gaze shifted to her. "Oh, I'll stop by the first day of the month to collect it."

She'd half expected he would give her a mailing address. But she shouldn't have been surprised that he intended to keep an eye on the place.

Hank snorted. "Don't you work, McKenna? Or do you just specialize in minding other people's business?"

That's what was different, Clancey thought, what had been nagging at her as she watched him. It was Thursday morning, and the ordinary professional man would be on his way to the office. But, in vibrant contrast to Hank's three-piece suit, Rowan was wearing jeans that were nowhere near new, sneakers, a faded flannel shirt and the almost inevitable cap.

"I *am* working," Rowan said mildly. "I'm a landlord now, too, on top of my other responsibilities. I'm just taking care of business—inspecting my property." He wandered into the parlor and stopped to study the teddy-bear tree. Or was it the mantel he was looking at? It was hard to tell.

"Well, some of us have more important things to do. Clancey, don't forget our date for Saturday night."

She blinked. "Saturday? Oh, the fund-raiser for the new civic center? But that's next week, surely, not two days from now."

"Oh, yes, that's what I meant. These tax hearings are going to tie me up all next week." He shot a look at Rowan and kissed Clancey's cheek. "Back to the grind, I'm afraid."

"Tax hearings?" Rowan said as soon as Hank was gone. "I warned him not to let his client take those deductions, but would Hank listen?" He shook his head.

"How would you know which client he's talking about?" Clancey asked.

"When you hang around city hall, you hear things. Are you making sales yet?"

"The doors actually don't open till tomorrow, but I wouldn't turn down cash if someone insisted. Why?"

"I need a teddy bear." He took the top one off the tree and brought it over to the cash register.

"That's my favorite bear in the whole store." Clancey gave the sad-eyed panda a last, almost surreptitious pat and carefully clipped the price tag from the loop at the back of his neck. "I'm a little sorry to see him go."

"It's a good cause." Rowan McKenna pulled a money clip from his pocket and pulled a bill loose. "He's going on a peacekeeping mission."

That's odd, she thought. Unless the bear was a gift for a child who was disappointed that he—or she— wouldn't be moving to a new house just yet, after all.

It was funny she'd never considered the possibility that Rowan McKenna was a father, or even a husband. But it made sense; a single man wasn't likely to be interested in a house the size of this one. What would he do with it all? And he was certainly eligible enough to be married, and old enough to be a father.

And also, she reminded herself, decent enough not to use a child's disappointment as a weapon to make her give up the house.

The stab of gratitude made her feel a little sentimental. She bundled the panda into a bag, turned back to the cash register and did one more calculation, and told him the cost. "I've given you a discount," she added. "Since this is the very first sale in my new location, you get a break."

Rowan shook his head sadly. "You can't keep on with that sort of thing," he warned. "You know how villainous landlords can be."

"I know—you'll tie me to a railroad track if I can't pay the rent."

He looked over her shoulder at the model train she'd just completed. "That's right. I see you've even got the track. How handy." He pulled a single sheet of paper out of his back pocket. "As long as we're talking about the rent, here's the new lease covering all the terms we talked about last night."

Clancey took it warily. Why hadn't he given her this when Hank was standing there? "You don't mind if I look it over and get back to you later?"

Rowan shrugged. "How long do you think it will be till Hank has adequate time to study it?"

"Oh, I'm sure he'll find a few minutes for me, even with the tax people hanging over him," she said sweetly.

Rowan only smiled and went out whistling with the panda tucked under his arm.

Eileen appeared with a stuffed leopard and began to arrange it on the stairway above Clancey's head.

"Too bad such a nice guy has to have a receding hairline," Eileen said, tugging the leopard's head between the balusters so it appeared to be guarding the cash register.

"You mean Rowan? He doesn't have a receding hairline."

"Isn't that why he wears that hat all the time?"

"No. And what are you complaining about, anyway? At least it's not a toupee."

"That's true." Eileen retied the leopard's red velvet bow. "You got onto a first-name basis awfully quickly."

Clancey had to run her memory back over the conversation before she realized that Eileen was right. When *had* she started thinking of Rowan by his first name?

"You were going to explain this system of yours to me," Eileen reminded her. She settled herself on the stairs just down from the leopard as if she intended to stay there till the promise was kept. "The one for finding men, I mean."

"I've decided it was no good."

Eileen stared at her. "It brings you masculine treats like Rowan McKenna and you're giving it up?"

"Men who buy stuffed panda bears are generally not what you'd call available, Eileen."

"And he's in that category? I knew it. All the good ones are taken, so I might as well not worry about it anymore." She dusted off the back of her slacks. "What's next?"

"Organizing the stockroom," Clancey was just starting to say when a noise interrupted her. It sounded like the front porch collapsing—a grinding, slithering, sliding noise that grated on her ears like a steak knife squealing across a plate. "What in the world was that?"

Eileen hadn't even jumped. "Oh, that's probably just Rowan on the roof. He was climbing a ladder by the front porch last time I saw him, so I assume—"

Clancey clenched her jaw. "And what is he doing on the roof?"

"Beats me. Maybe you should ask him."

The front door had jammed again. Clancey gave up on it and headed for the window on the hexagonal landing at the head of the stairs, overlooking the porch roof.

Sure enough, Rowan was crouched on the asphalt surface, a pry bar in his hand, yanking pieces of the roof loose. The sound she'd heard was old shingles sliding down and falling into heaps in the flower beds around the porch.

She struggled to open the window, but it, like every other one she'd tried, had been painted shut. So she rapped on the glass to get his attention.

He looked up and waved cheerfully.

Clancey yelled, "What do you think you're doing?"

"Checking out the bad spots in the roof," he called back, moving over to the window.

She bit her tongue and then pointed out as calmly as she could. "I'm having a grand opening starting tomorrow. Remember?"

"Certainly I remember. I told you the roof needed work, didn't I? You don't want your customers to get rained on, do you?"

Clancey swallowed hard. "The roof leaks that badly?"

"Obviously you haven't been in the attic. There's water damage all over the place."

Her voice was rising. "Are you seriously going to tear the roof off this house today?"

"Not all of it."

She closed her eyes in pain.

"I'm just taking a couple of layers off the porch to see how far the roofers will have to go. I want to speed the job along so it's done before the bad weather."

Clancey gritted her teeth till her jaw ached. Finally she was able to say politely, "You do realize that you agreed to leave the house entirely in my possession till January, don't you? And it's not January yet."

He shrugged. "Be reasonable, Clancey. I can't replace the roof in January. It will be too snowy, too cold and too windy. Besides, you've got the inside all to yourself. What else do you want?"

What she wanted right then was a window that opened. If she had one, she could've climbed out onto the roof herself and pushed him off.

THE FIRST DAY OF Clancey's grand opening was a perfect autumn Friday, the kind that kindergartners were apt to draw. There were puffy white clouds in a perfect blue sky, yellows and red and oranges of all shades draped across the trees, and the still-green grass was like a carpet.

It was almost as if Mother Nature had decided to deck herself out in brilliant crayon colors just to complement Small World's sign, Clancey thought a little giddily as she checked the front of the house one last time. Yes, the sign was still there, straight and easy to see, hanging on the porch rail. Yes, the sidewalk was swept clean. Yes, the lawn was free of obstacles; amazingly, Rowan had cleaned up his own mess yesterday before he'd gone away.

Best of all, there were a few cars pulling in along Pine Street and people were getting out and coming up the walk to Small World. As the morning wore on, the numbers grew.

It was busier than she'd anticipated for the first day. She'd allowed herself to hope for good traffic over the weekend, but she'd expected to be able to work out any glitches in the system before the rush began. However, both she and Eileen were run off their feet, and by midmorning Clancey was beginning to feel that if she could manage to look up and smile when the front door opened she was doing well.

That was about the time the florist's van double-parked in front of the house and the delivery man lifted a big vase of cut flowers from the back. He had some trouble negotiating his way across the crowded porch and through the door, for attached to the vase with long ribbons were more than a dozen helium-filled balloons reaching for the heavens.

It wasn't the only good-luck bouquet Clancey had received, but it was certainly the biggest and the brightest, and it piqued her curiosity. She managed to find a moment between boxing up a doll and guiding a young mother to the cassette tapes to tear open the envelope that nestled between a brilliant red carnation and a huge yellow mum.

"Good luck in your new location," the printed card said. That was standard enough, but in red ink across the bottom was neatly written, "I look forward to doing this again in January."

There was no name, of course, but who needed one? The red ink alone would have told Clancey all she had to know—of course an accountant would have plenty of that on hand!

She carried a dollhouse kit out to a car for the customer who'd bought it—for herself, the woman confided, not for her grandchildren—and seized the opportunity to get a breath of air. Pine Street was still so busy that she began to wonder if there would be enough parking at peak times.

Then Clancey laughed. *What a problem,* she chided herself. *Unfortunately I won't have it for long....*

In a slightly chastened mood, she turned back toward the store and stopped to let a group of customers pass. Otherwise she might not have noticed the woman coming slowly down the sidewalk.

She was about Clancey's age, with a long champagne-blond braid down her back and an infant in a sling on her chest. She stopped directly in front of the house and stared up at it with a tiny frown between her eyebrows.

The look on the woman's face startled Clancey. She couldn't quite identify it. It couldn't be confusion about Small World, she thought. With the big sign on the porch and people coming and going there could be no doubt about where the entrance was. It didn't seem to be annoyance, either, as it might have been if a neighbor was upset with this sudden increase in traffic. It certainly wasn't anything as strong as anger. And simple puzzlement made no sense....

In any case, it didn't matter, and Clancey settled for smiling pleasantly at the woman. The moment she was back inside Eileen threw her a harassed look, and feeling guilty, Clancey plunged into the parlor again and began trying to help customers two and three at a time. The blonde on the sidewalk was forgotten.

It was perhaps twenty minutes later when a woman caught Clancey's arm. "You're the owner?" she asked. "I live next door. Glad to see someone in the place again."

Hoping the neighbor would take the hint, Clancey briefly smiled her thanks and looked over the woman's shoulder to the next customer. It was the blonde, and she was standing in the double doorway of the sun porch, looking at mobiles to hang above a baby's crib.

But the neighbor's hand was firm on Clancey's elbow. "Lots of work to be done here, isn't there?" Her voice might have been meant to be confidential, but it carried above the buzz of talk in the parlor. "I heard the argument you had with your workman yesterday."

"Oh, did you?" Clancey asked repressively.

The woman grinned. "I was covering my roses, you see," she confided. "I couldn't help but hear, the way you were both yelling. It's hard to get good help these days, isn't it?"

"It certainly is," Clancey agreed. "Now if you'll excuse me..."

She noticed a smile tugging at the corner of the blonde's mouth, and told herself that it was unreasonable to be annoyed simply because the woman seemed to find her amusing. And letting annoyance stand in the way of serving the customer wasn't good business, either.

Clancey took a deep breath. "That's a very popular mobile. There are different sets of toys to hang from it, too, so the baby doesn't get bored with looking at it."

The blonde nodded and handed over the box. "That's a good recommendation," she murmured. "Though at the moment it seems impossible that this little boy will ever manage to stay awake long enough to be bored."

Clancey stole a glance at the infant in the sling. The small face was perfectly bland, wiped clean of expression by the soundness of his sleep. His soft skin still had the peculiar bluish transparency of the newborn, particularly around his eyelids. Clancey's fingers itched to touch the soft fuzz of dark hair, but she restrained herself. "How old is he?" she asked as she rang up the sale.

"Six days. This is his first official outing, and look at him—he's missing it all." The blonde tugged a wallet from the diaper bag hanging from her shoulder.

"Be sure to put your name in the barrel. The prize is a handmade wooden rocking horse, and this little guy will be needing one before you can imagine." While the blonde was filling out the entry slip to drop in the barrel, Clancey took a quick look at her check, automatically noting that it was drawn on a local bank. It wasn't until she read the name that she got the shock; neat block letters printed on the green slip of paper announced that the blonde's last name was McKenna.

Well, Clancey thought, *some things would be obvious if you had the slightest powers of observation, Kincade!*

The blonde had been standing on the sidewalk staring at the house. Once inside, she'd probably been looking not only at mobiles but at the sun porch itself. And that baby boy she was carrying certainly hadn't gotten his fuzz of dark hair from his mother.

No wonder the woman had been amused; she must have found the idea of Rowan as an ordinary workman hysterically funny.

Clancey glanced at the check again. *Kaye McKenna.* The name had a nice rhythm to it.

It was a name that Clancey supposed she ought to have expected to hear, sooner or later. If Rowan hadn't seen the house, then his wife probably hadn't, either. She'd be just as curious about it as he had been, and just as likely to take an opportunity to get a look, even if she had to buy a toy in the room she'd hoped to be arranging her furniture in by now.

"If you'd like to take a look around the house," Clancey said, "feel free, Mrs. McKenna."

There was a momentary gleam of surprise in the blonde's eyes, as if she'd expected to be thrown bodily out rather than invited to stay. Then she said, "Thank you. I'd love to see it. But surely some other day would be better for a tour, when you're not so busy?" She smiled and gathered up her purchase and the diaper bag, slipping out the front door before Clancey could say another word.

Clancey was absolutely dumbfounded. Why had the woman turned down the opportunity to wander around?

Eileen reached over her shoulder to ring up a sale and growled, "What's gotten into you? Give one person a tour and everybody will want one."

"I hadn't thought of that," Clancey managed to say.

But Kaye McKenna must have. It was the only possible explanation for her turning down the offer—that it was likely to cause difficulty for Clancey.

The woman has class, she found herself thinking.

There was no reason on earth why that simple fact should upset Clancey. But it certainly did.

CHAPTER FOUR

LONG AFTER KAYE MCKENNA and her son had left Small World, Clancey found herself thinking about them. So her intuition about Rowan's buying the panda had been right, after all. That precious baby boy, six days old, was the new owner of the toy Clancey had liked so much—or was he?

It didn't really make sense, when she stopped to think about it. Surely such a tiny infant, so sweetly oblivious of everything about him, couldn't have prompted anything like a peacekeeping mission. Perhaps Rowan had been referring to Kaye herself, and her undoubted disappointment—but in that case a panda seemed an unlikely apology. Perhaps there was another child—one who was old enough to reason with, and old enough to feel cheated and angry. Just because there was a baby didn't mean there couldn't be another child. A girl, perhaps, old enough to be in school....

Oh, for heaven's sake! Clancey told herself helplessly. How many kids Rowan McKenna might have— or their respective states of mind—was certainly none of her business. She needed a little catch-up sleep and a whole lot of common sense, that was all.

But the grand opening meant no time for either. The heavy work of moving boxes and crates had left her stiff and sore. The cruel hours she'd been keeping had drained her stamina. Worst of all, the blow of finding that her dream was to be only a fleeting illusion slashed away the hope and joy that had made the hard work and the hours bearable.

But at least she'd finally found the missing rail of her brass bed, so—short as the night had been—she'd managed her first decent sleep in a week. Still, it was no wonder she groaned when the sun came over the horizon; she had to think of caffeine in large doses in order to make herself get up.

Clancey was sitting at the kitchen table, a coffee mug clutched between her hands, gathering her strength to deal with customers again in an hour, when Rowan knocked on the back door.

She wasn't surprised. He hadn't shown up in nearly forty-eight hours, and his absence had been too good to be true.

"I expected you'd still be back here," he said with a self-congratulatory note in his voice.

"Great." Clancey sighed. "Yours is just the lovely smiling face I was longing to see this morning."

"Really?" He appeared to be rather flattered at the idea.

She glared at him. "All right, I admit it's too early in the morning for sarcasm. So what do you want today?"

Rowan shrugged and moved into the kitchen. He was wearing jeans even older than the ones he'd worn to crawl around on the porch roof, and he was carrying a very large container of coffee. "Have you had a chance to sign the lease?"

"Not yet." She looked him over suspiciously. "Why insist on a lease, anyway, for just a couple of months?

Why isn't a handshake good enough? Don't you trust me?"

"Not as far as I could—" he began, and then shook his head a little and grinned. "I like to have things tidy, that's all."

"I'll just bet that's all it is," Clancey muttered. "So I plan to study that lease of yours very thoroughly. Who knows what you've got hidden in the fine print?"

Rowan shrugged again. "Let Hank read it. I don't care."

"That's what frightens me. Whatever it is must be very well hidden if you think Hank can't find it. I suppose I should thank you for the flowers, by the way."

"Don't mention it. I understand it's customary for the landlord to send a bouquet on important occasions—openings, closings—"

"Don't waste your money in January," Clancey recommended dryly. "I've already got the message."

"But it will be my pleasure." His eyes brightened. "Unless you sell everything during the grand opening and want to go ahead and move out sooner. If that's why you'd rather not sign the lease, I'd be happy to amend it to let you leave earlier."

"Don't bet on it happening."

Rowan sighed, and the gleam faded from his eyes. "I'm not. I never was lucky at gambling."

There was a bang against the side of the house that sent Clancey six inches into the air. Rowan strolled over to the window. "Oh, here's my crew."

"The roofers?" she said. "Already?"

"No, they don't work on weekends. This is the painters."

"You're going to paint *today?*" Her voice was a bit shrill.

He smiled kindly. "Yes—isn't it a lovely day? The paint will dry in no time."

"It's my grand opening," she said through gritted teeth.

"I seem to remember you telling me that. Don't worry, the inside is still all yours, and we'll try to stay out of your way. But I had to take them when I could get them, you see."

"On Saturday?"

"Yes, that's exactly what I mean. All my friends are pitching in to help me now that I need a hand. We're amateurs when it comes to paint, of course, but it's a rather large crew, so we should be done in only a couple of weekends."

He looked very proud of himself. Clancey knew better than to think she could maneuver fast enough to stop him. He'd simply point out that he certainly couldn't paint in January when he got full possession of the house, and how could she argue about that? Nor could she say the house didn't need the attention; she'd be laughed off the block if she tried to defend its present condition and faded, peeling, mustard yellow facade.

"What color is it going to be?" she asked finally. Her voice didn't sound quite normal.

He obviously recognized she was surrendering, but it didn't seem to matter to him. "Sort of pink and blue. Kaye picked the colors, because she's much better at it than I am."

No doubt, Clancey thought, but she said, "That will be a nice touch for my business. Very appropriate."

The emerald sparkle she was beginning to recognize came back into his eyes as he said solemnly, "I promise we'll all be very careful not to drip on your customers.''

Clancey released a small strangled noise. Then she jumped up, dumped the dregs of her coffee and put the cup in the sink. On the chipped old porcelain drain board lay yesterday's mail and the bill the locksmith had handed her after he'd managed to unjam the front door. She'd been planning to pay it herself rather than make waves with an unwilling landlord, but if the man was going to make a nuisance of himself like this, he might as well learn to pay the piper.

Sheer annoyance made her pick up the bill and thrust it at Rowan. "Since you're so eager to fix everything that's wrong with the outside of this house, this obviously belongs to you, too."

He glanced at it and looked at her thoughtfully. "Ah, yes. Thank you. I'll take care of my share, of course."

Clancey's jaw dropped. "What do you mean, your share?"

"My half."

"Half? You're the landlord. That makes you responsible for the physical surroundings."

"I wouldn't dare interfere with the inside. That's yours. And precisely half of the door is on the inside." He started toward the back porch.

"Now wait a minute." Clancey was beginning to steam. "You're not getting out of this as easily as that. There are rules—" She bit her tongue, too late. If she kept it up, he'd probably swear that she'd encouraged him to start tearing out the walls and the plumbing!

"Really?" He sounded interested. "I'm so new to this landlord business, you see, that I haven't any idea how the rules work. Now that you mention it, I believe the matter of who pays the bills when something breaks is covered in the lease—but of course since you haven't signed it . . ."

"And since, at this rate, I'm not going to," Clancey muttered, "you might as well give me back the damned bill. Forget I ever mentioned it, all right?"

"Oh, no," Rowan said with an air of scrupulous fairness. "I'll certainly take care of my share." He folded the paper, tucked it into his hip pocket and went outside. A few minutes later she heard the first scratch of a paint scraper by the kitchen window. She supposed that as soon as the shop opened, he'd move his ladder to the front door.

"Just what I needed," she muttered. "As if I didn't already have a headache."

ROWAN HADN'T BEEN KIDDING about having a sizable crew. At midafternoon Clancey finished helping a customer strap a playhouse-sized kitchen set atop his compact car and turned back toward the house without a thought for anything but the people waiting inside. The changed appearance of the house made her blink in surprise; the entire front wall had already been washed with new color.

Sort of pink and blue, indeed! she thought. Wasn't that just like a man? It was fortunate he'd left the choice of paint colors to someone else, that was certain.

Most of the siding was now the soft creamy blue of an Impressionist landscape, but the shingles covering the second story were warm mauve. A darker blue picked out the delicate tracery around the windows, and here and there a touch of off-white accented a detail. Around both corners of the house she could see ladders planted against the side walls and painters going up and down, agile as monkeys and seemingly never getting in each other's way.

Rowan came around the corner with a big bucket and set it in the back of a pickup truck. He saw her, Clancey was certain of that, but he made no comment, just started to get behind the wheel.

She almost kept silent, too, then told herself that sometimes simple decency paid off in the long run. There couldn't be anything wrong with paying a sincere compliment, could there? So she called across the lawn to him, "It looks great! At this rate it won't take a couple of weekends, surely."

Rowan shrugged. "So far, it's moving along well, but of course it will slow down when we have to stop and haul water for the cleanup tonight."

"Haul— You mean you've been driving somewhere to get water by the bucket just to clean brushes and things?" She bit her lip. "You could have asked to use my kitchen."

"You could have offered," he pointed out. "Since you didn't, I assumed you didn't want to be bothered."

"I didn't think about it. Look, I'm not completely unreasonable, Rowan. Help yourself to water—to whatever you need. Just use the back door, all right?"

His face didn't change expression. "You're certain you don't mind the mess?"

"Don't be ridiculous," she snapped. "Of course I mind. But you can use the kitchen anyway."

It wasn't until later that she realized she might well find her kitchen in ruins, and that she couldn't say much about it because she'd technically given permission for any sort of chaos he might create.

By the time the shop closed, it was dark and the painting crew was gone. Eileen finished vacuuming the parlor and said, "I'll come in early tomorrow if you like and help stock the shelves before we open. But I'm going out for dinner tonight with a man, so..."

Clancey looked up from the cash register where she was tallying the day's receipts. "You're kidding. I thought you said you were finished with all that nonsense."

"I said I wasn't going to look for a man anymore. And that's absolutely true."

"Then how do you account for a dinner date?"

"He ran over my foot with a grocery cart in the frozen-foods aisle at the supermarket."

Clancey shook her head in confusion. "And that means he doesn't count as a date?"

"Of course not," Eileen said airily. "If I'd been looking for a date, I'd have seen him coming and I wouldn't have been injured."

Only after Eileen blew her a kiss and left did Clancey allow herself to chuckle. When the inevitable time came, Eileen would probably poke her head up out of her casket just to see whether the undertaker was worth going after!

She finished up the receipts and wearily headed for the kitchen, braced for whatever she might find. Blue and mauve paint spattered on the walls? Water sprayed all over? Buckets and brushes on every flat surface?

But the only evidence that her kitchen had been used was a neat pile of brushes drying in an out-of-the-way corner on the back porch.

Clancey decided that she'd actually have been less annoyed if they *had* left the place in a shambles. As it was, she was furious at Rowan. Did he really think her so rigid that she'd put others to extra work just for the principle of the thing?

But that was probably exactly what he thought. Because, in his view, if she didn't think that way she wouldn't still be in the house, keeping him from enjoying his property!

ON SUNDAYS SMALL WORLD didn't open till noon, but the painters were out in force as soon as the sun had climbed high enough to banish the frost that had accumulated overnight. Some of them were there even before Rowan was, and when he arrived and saw a group of them with doughnuts in hand, and Clancey with her coffeepot refilling mugs, his eyebrows rose so high they almost disappeared under the brim of his cap. "What brought this on?"

His surprise annoyed her. "It was the least I could do to thank everybody for not dropping loaded paintbrushes on my customers yesterday," she said tartly. She pushed a coffee mug into his hand, wishing she dared pour the hot brew over his fingers instead of into the cup.

He stayed behind for a moment after the others had all gone off to the ladders. "Look, I'm sorry I put it that way. I'll be happy to pay you back for the coffee and doughnuts. It's my crew, and my responsibility to feed them."

She shrugged. She didn't look at him, but her tone was a little softer. "That's not necessary. They're doing me a favor, too. My customers seem to like the new color scheme."

There was a short pause. "Then I'll just say thanks. It was very thoughtful of you, Clancey."

The note of approval in his voice made Clancey nervous, and she turned her back and began to gather up the empty mugs. "Where did you find all these people, anyway?"

"I help out my friends when they need something, so now they're helping me."

She looked at him appraisingly. "You've got lots of friends."

He shrugged it off. "I've always been sort of handy with tools. It all balances out in the end." He reached for a doughnut and smiled at her across its chocolate-coated surface. "I was too tired last night even to stick around and thank you for letting us use the water. I should have. I'm sorry I didn't."

His smile was a slow, steady stream of charm, and there was no teasing emerald glint in his eyes, either—only pure, deep blue sincerity. The combination was just short of deadly; it made Clancey feel as if ordinary air wouldn't quite fit the shape of her lungs anymore, and so there was no sense in trying to breathe.

The man is dangerous, Clancey thought. His wife ought to know better than to let him loose on an unsuspecting world full of women.

Fortunately he went off to paint a moment later, before she could pass out from lack of oxygen.

The traffic through Small World was slower today, with fewer but larger sales. Off and on all through the afternoon the customers commented about the new look of the house. Clancey had learned to listen with half her attention, smiling and nodding a lot, which took care of most of the remarks.

But about midafternoon a tall woman wearing a designer suit brought a fashion doll up to the cash register and said, "You will agree to be part of the neighborhood Christmas tour of houses this year, won't you, Miss Kincade?" Her tone implied there was no doubt about the answer, because no one had the bad taste to refuse such a rare invitation.

Another thing to do before Christmas, Clancey thought automatically before she realized that even if it had sounded like a royal decree, she could still turn down the honor. So she made the first excuse that came into her head. "Isn't that only for the actual historic district? I'm a couple of blocks outside the edge of that, so I'm afraid no matter how much I wanted to join in, it wouldn't be quite—"

The woman waved a dismissive hand. "Oh, that's nothing. We're always politicking to get the area expanded. But I'll talk to our chairman and make certain there won't be a problem. You know her, I imagine—everybody who cares about old houses knows Kaye McKenna." She smiled. "We're so glad to have you join us, Miss Kincade."

I can manage to get myself into trouble, Clancey thought, *without even trying.* If she only hadn't made it sound as if she was longing for the opportunity....

She thought about it quite a lot through the rest of the afternoon. As a matter of fact, the idea of a Christmas open house appealed to her a great deal. She'd have the store decorated anyway, and would make it a point to stay open for whatever hours the tour involved, whether she was part of it or not. The exposure and publicity would be good for Small World; anyone who walked in the door, even if it was to admire woodwork or architectural detail, was a potential customer.

But the attraction for Clancey was a great deal more than that. After all, it had been the summer neighborhood tour that had drawn her here in the first place and fixed her attention on the idea of converting an old house. It was only natural to want to show off her own place—

Except that it wasn't her own place, and she wouldn't be able even to pretend that it was for much longer. In December, when her neighbors were enjoying the Christmas tour, Clancey would be preparing to close the shop and looking frantically for somewhere else to go.

It almost made her cry, to have to admit how much she would have loved being a part of the Christmas tour, if only circumstances had been different. This house could be perfect at Christmastime, garlanded in pine and ribbon, sprinkled with antique toys, lighted with candles and tiny twinkling bulbs.

She swallowed the lump in her throat and reminded herself that no doubt next year the house would be open for tours. If Kaye McKenna was already in charge of the whole event, her own house would certainly be a part of it just as soon as she could manage.

Maybe I'll come back and look at it, Clancey thought. And then she laughed a little at her own idiocy, and retreated to the stockroom for a moment to dry her eyes and try to get herself under control.

THE PAINTERS WORKED LATE, but the house was almost done when the crew left that night. When Clancey completed the week's book work and wandered into the kitchen to find herself something to eat, the only one left was Rowan, still cleaning brushes in the sink.

"It's getting late," she pointed out, digging the raw materials for a sandwich out of the refrigerator.

"Sorry," he said. "I'll be out of your way as soon as I can, but if these things aren't cleaned tonight they'll be ruined."

Clancey shrugged. "So clean them. Want a sandwich?"

He looked surprised. "Sure."

She couldn't keep herself from yawning now and then as she ate her sandwich and watched as he snatched bites between brushes. There were a dozen of them yet to be cleaned, in all sizes, and the paint swirled down the drain in rainbows of blue and mauve and cream as he patiently worked water through the bristles.

"You look as if you've done that a lot," she said. It wasn't that she cared, actually, she told herself, but the silence was wearing on her.

He looked up as if surprised by the half question. "I earned my spending money all the way through college by painting houses during the summer."

"I should think you'd have your fill of it by now."

He grinned. "Oh, now it's purely a hobby. I do it just often enough so that whenever I'm auditing a set of books and start to see double, I can remind myself of the way my muscles ache after a day on an extension ladder with a scraper." He demonstrated the arm movement, and winced a little. "It makes the auditing a whole lot easier to bear."

"I'll bet." He had plenty of muscles to ache, Clancey thought half-consciously, and then asked herself in surprise just when she'd had time to notice. It was true, though; she could see the ripple of strength through his shoulders and arms.

He was watching her with interest. "I've been wondering, Clancey. What got you into toys, anyway?"

She answered with the same kind of lightness. "I've been accused of having a juvenile fixation, which only intensive psychotherapy could fix. I've also been told that I'm caught in a mental war between wanting children and not wanting them, so this is my way of soothing the desire, while ensuring I'm left no time to act on it. But in fact—"

He shook his head. "Don't tell me. The truth is that you like to play with them yourself."

Clancey smiled. "Yeah. I started buying wooden puzzles and mechanical toys at flea markets years ago, and this is where I ended up. I'll probably be the only parent in history who owns more playthings than my kids ever will."

"So you do want children?"

"I suppose so, some day. There are a few other things I'd need first, you know."

He smiled at that.

The tenderness of the expression reminded her of the tiny baby boy he must be thinking of. It made her feel a little awkward, wanting to mention the baby, to tell him what a precious child he had. But she couldn't seem to find a natural way to do it, and so she faked another yawn instead, in the hope that he'd take the hint. "Excuse me, but it's been an awfully long week."

"I'll be done here in a few minutes. Go on to bed if you like. I'll finish up and lock the door."

"Goodness, doesn't that sound domestic?" She managed a laugh, to make it clear she hadn't intended a double meaning, and retreated up the back stairs. She could at least brush her teeth while she waited for him to leave, before going back down to lock the dead bolts.

She took more time with her nightly ritual than usual. Her moisturizing cream had never been so carefully applied, or her dental floss so conscientiously used. By the time she was finished, the house was going through *its* regular ritual of creaks and moans. She was getting used to all that noise, finally. The first couple of nights it had scared her silly. But now she knew it was only the structure adjusting itself as daytime heat gave way to night's cooler temperatures.

She started into her bedroom to turn the blankets down. It was the prettiest of the rooms, with handgrained wood trim and a curved alcove lined with lead glass windows. It was big and airy and pleasant, and her grandmother's brass bed fit perfectly at an angle opposite the alcove. The walls should be papered in a sunny yellow print, she thought, with white eyelet curtains—but of course that was out of the question now.

She was in the doorway when the house gave one more convulsive groan. In what seemed to Clancey like slow motion, most of the plaster ceiling broke loose from its supports and dropped, to shatter and splinter and well up in a choking cloud of dust. Much of it landed on top of the bed, where—if not for Rowan McKenna and his pesky paintbrushes—Clancey would have been sleeping, blissfully unconscious of the danger hovering above her.

At this moment, she realized in horror, she would have been buried under a half ton of plaster. And she might very well have been dead.

CHAPTER FIVE

THE DUST WAS THICK and blinding. Clancey managed to retreat a couple of feet and stood helplessly on the landing, choking and coughing. She heard Rowan running up the back stairs, and she turned and flung herself against him so hard that his breath was driven out in a sudden whoosh. Clancey didn't notice that; the only sensation she had was of warm, strong arms closing around her, promising to keep her safe.

"Are you all right?" he demanded finally.

Clancey nodded, her head buried against Rowan's shoulder as if she was an ostrich and he a convenient sand dune. His flannel shirt was soft and warm against her face, and the scents that clung to it—of crisp fall air and paint and smoke from someone's burning leaves—filled her nose. His hand gently touched the back of her head and then slipped down the length of her hair. It was almost an absentminded stroking, but it was no less sensual for that. It would have sent shudders through Clancey's bones if she hadn't had her mind fixed on other things at the moment.

Rowan looked over her shoulder into the bedroom, where the dust had begun to settle and the gaping cavity in the ceiling was now apparent through the thinning haze.

"Aren't you glad you agreed to let me fix the roof?" he said. He sounded a little breathless.

She turned her head. "That wasn't the roof." Her voice held a small quaver. "Was it?"

"No, but the ceiling's probably been waterlogged somewhere along the line. And now that the boiler's been turned on again, after two years without heat—well, it would be a wonder if something hadn't cracked somewhere."

His hands began to move up and down her back again in a soothing massage. The touch felt good against her tense muscles, and it was a full minute before Clancey realized that it wasn't the wisest place to rest—snuggled against him like a lover, right outside her bedroom door. What if he thought her calm acceptance was some kind of invitation?

Though, she reminded herself, only a nut could find anything sexually appealing about that bedroom just now. And as for Clancey herself, she could still smell the dust and feel the grit on her face. In fact, she could almost taste it. No, there was nothing sexually appealing about her at the moment, either.

Still, for safety's sake, she planted both hands against his chest and pushed herself away.

Rowan didn't make any move to hold her. He folded his arms across his chest. "Feeling better?"

"A little, yes. It was a closer call than I would have chosen." She stepped over to the bedroom, peering in.

Rowan caught at her arm. "Don't go in there. The rest might fall at any minute."

"I wasn't planning to, exactly. It's just that my nightshirt is in there, and my pillow—"

"And that's where you'd better leave them until someone's taken a crowbar to the rest of the loose plaster. Look, why don't you just come home with me? Let the dust settle and worry about it tomorrow."

She glared at him.

Rowan winced and said defensively, "Well, at least you'd have a clean place to sleep. Don't look at me that way, Clancey. I'm certainly not making a pass."

"Of course you're not," Clancey said coolly, unwilling to admit the idea had even crossed her mind. There wasn't a lot of comfort in the knowledge that he agreed with her less-than-flattering assessment of herself at the moment. Then she remembered that he did, after all, have someone waiting for him at home, and she wasted a few moments imagining what Kaye's reaction was likely to be if he turned up at this hour with a bedraggled female in tow. How would he explain that one, she wondered. Like a child with a stray animal? Hi, honey. She followed me home—can I keep her?

"Thanks," she said stiffly, "but I'll just bed down here. I left some blankets in the living room from the last night I spent on the floor. I'll be all right."

"Whatever you like." Rowan was equally polite. "I just hope the rest of the ceilings aren't loose."

He poked around at them until Clancey was so nervous she was ready to scream, then announced that everything looked safe enough for the moment and departed. It was much later before she had calmed down enough to settle into her makeshift bed. Even then, she didn't fall asleep quickly. The memory of that crushing load of falling plaster played itself over and over in her head every time she shut her eyes.

And when she did manage to banish that image, she found her face burning at the memory of how she'd thrown herself into Rowan's arms and pressed against him and let him stroke her like a lover.

It was guilt. That was what was nagging at her, she decided finally. She felt guilty for acting that way with a married man.

It was stupid, of course, to be feeling any such thing. She'd been in shock, and his actions had—mostly—been in the nature of a rescue. She certainly hadn't flung herself at him on purpose, and she'd never do it again, even if she wanted to, which of course she didn't.

Guilt. What an insane thing to be feeling!

CLANCEY DIDN'T UNDERSTAND why fate should have suddenly turned against her, but that was what seemed to be happening. On Monday morning when she opened the registration barrel and drew a name for the winner of the grand opening prize, she pulled out the card that said Kaye McKenna. Before she could help herself she swore a streak that made Eileen look respectful, and then curious.

It was the curiosity that stopped Clancey midword. It was ridiculous to be upset over something so unimportant, Clancey told herself. So what if she had spent a few minutes huddled in Rowan's arms? No one could begrudge her that, after the close escape she'd had. As she'd told herself a hundred times last night, she had nothing to feel guilty about.

"You could just draw another name," Eileen suggested.

Clancey dialed the telephone number before Eileen could pursue the matter, and invited Kaye to come for tea late that afternoon to collect her prize.

Eileen was watching her speculatively when she put the telephone down. "She's coming?"

"Are you surprised? If I wasn't being polite, I'd say the invitation was snapped up with unladylike haste."

"Well, that should make it easier to exploit the situation."

Clancey blinked in astonishment. "What do you mean? I happened to draw her registration card, that's all. I'm not exploiting—"

"Not that I'd blame you if you had rigged the winner. But it didn't take you long to see the advantages, did it? You're hoping that when Kaye McKenna sees that hole in the ceiling she'll start to wonder what else is wrong with this house, and maybe she'll decide she doesn't want to touch the place, after all. And then you'll get to finish out your lease. Right?"

Clancey hadn't thought that far ahead, as a matter of fact. But as soon as she stopped marveling over Eileen's Machiavellian turn of mind, she began to wonder if Eileen might be right. This whole thing could possibly work to her advantage.

She hadn't swept up the pile of fallen plaster in her bedroom. Now that the dust had settled, the sight was even more daunting than it had been last night. A network of cracks spread like a massive spiderweb across the remaining plaster, and huge chunks sagged at the edges of the hole, defying gravity—at least for the moment.

Kaye McKenna would have to possess nerves of steel to look at that mess without qualms. And if she was to change her mind about the house...

Clancey was actually smiling when she answered the front door a half hour after closing time. Her first sight of Kaye McKenna added to her rather guilty satisfaction; the blonde was wearing a slacks suit in a nubby dark green fabric that would be a perfect magnet for plaster dust.

"Am I too early?" she asked, eyeing Clancey's apron.

"Not at all. If you don't mind waiting for the kettle to boil, that is. I had a customer right at closing time."

Kaye smiled. "May I help?"

Translated, Clancey thought, that simply meant she couldn't wait to see the rest of the house.

She led the way to the kitchen and rescued a pan of cookies from the oven just moments before they would have started to burn. "Does that happen often?" Kaye asked. "The last-minute customer, I mean."

Clancey made a face. "Often enough. If it was just ordinary things I wouldn't mind, but generally it's a parent who put off buying a birthday present for his kid until fifteen minutes before the party starts, and now he needs the world's most perfect toy. It's going to be the worst part of living here, too. I had no idea how many people were pounding on my door after closing hours."

"Because you weren't there to hear them."

"Exactly. Now some people assume that I'm always open for business." Clancey began to set a tray with delicate china. "I thought perhaps you'd bring the baby."

"I decided it would be better not to bring him into the construction zone. So his father is showing him off to his clients this afternoon." Kaye sounded a little rueful. "That must be the original kitchen range, don't you think?"

"I imagine so. It works fine, too, which is more than can be said for the one in the upstairs kitchen. Feel free to look around all you like, Mrs. McKenna."

"Oh, call me Kaye, please. And thank you. I love to poke around old houses."

Especially this one, Clancey thought.

"I'll be careful of the ceilings, though. That must have been quite a surprise for you last night."

Clancey stopped arranging napkins and teacups. Kaye sounded very calm about it. She reminded herself it was easy to underestimate a mess one hadn't yet seen.

As she led the way up the main stairs to the hexagonal landing, she noticed that Kaye rubbed a loving hand over the stair rail.

"That banister is probably filthy," Clancey warned. "I haven't had a chance to clean anything, and the way the dust billowed up last night it probably didn't miss a corner." She jerked her head toward the open bedroom door, not surprised when Kaye immediately went over to look in.

Clancey took her time arranging the tray on the low table by the windows overlooking the porch roof. She wasn't certain what she was waiting for—an exclamation of shock, perhaps, followed by silent, wide-eyed abhorrence as the woman realized the extent of the damage.

If so, she was disappointed. Kaye turned away from the door and came to seat herself on a low chair. "It's fortunate you hadn't gone to bed yet," she said calmly. "How are you going to manage now?"

The woman was inhuman, Clancey thought, before remembering that if Kaye McKenna specialized in old houses, this must not be the first fallen ceiling she'd ever seen. Or was the woman simply pretending serenity?

If that was so, the best response was surely to put on a calm act of her own. Clancey picked up the teapot and shrugged. "I don't know. Fortunately I haven't yet had the time to get truly organized, so most of my clean clothes were still in the living room. Milk and sugar in your tea?"

"Just lemon. This house would certainly make an interesting exhibit for the Christmas tour, wouldn't it?"

She's fishing, Clancey told herself. *Seeing if I'm going to make a fool of myself.* "I hardly think it's suitable for that, in this condition."

"Oh, but you're wrong. People could see the kind of work really involved in restoration. Most of the houses on the tour are finished now, so all that's visible is the beauty, not the effort it took to get there."

"So visitors don't understand all that goes into the job," Clancey said. "I can certainly appreciate that point of view. If I'd known what I was getting into—" She bit her tongue. That wasn't quite what she'd intended to say.

Kaye reached for a cookie. "I understand you're concerned about being outside the historical district, but we're working on getting that changed. We'd like to see the preservation zone expanded so it takes in the entire neighborhood, right to the edge of the commercial section." She set her cup down and leaned forward confidentially. "Having you on the Christmas tour would be a great argument."

And it would help get the zoning change made before you move in, Clancey thought. She couldn't blame the woman for trying. She might have done the same thing, if she were in Kaye McKenna's shoes. "I'd like to help, but . . ."

Kaye seized on the hesitation. "How about putting out petitions asking for the expansion, and thinking about the tour?"

It was a good cause, Clancey reminded herself. For the sake of the house—all the houses in the neighborhood—she could put aside her usual reluctance to get involved in anything even vaguely political. "I'll help with petitions. But not the tour, since I'm really only going to be here a short while."

The sound of a fist hammering on the front door echoed up the stairs. Clancey thought about ignoring it, but knew that wouldn't be possible for long. Besides, it provided a graceful way to change the subject. "You see?" she said ruefully. "There's another one."

Couldn't people read? she thought fretfully as she ran down the stairs. Small World's hours were quite clearly posted right next to the door.

But of course the man who was knocking wasn't concerned about her business hours. "Haven't you gotten the doorbell fixed yet?" Rowan asked.

"No. It's on the outside of the house."

"Only the button. All the wires and connections and transformers and noisemakers, on the other hand, are—"

"I like my privacy. When there's no doorbell, most people give up and go away."

"Well, perhaps there's a better answer."

"What?" Clancey said dryly, eyeing the iron bar balanced across his shoulder. "The pry bar you're carrying? What project have you got in mind today, anyway?"

He imitated a fencer's pose, wielding the pry bar like a rapier. "Just call me the defender of a maiden's right to uninterrupted sleep in her own bed."

Clancey retreated a few steps, out of the pry bar's range. "I'll bet," she muttered.

Rowan paused at the top of the stairs, casting a surprised look at her guest. "Hello, Kaye. What are you doing here? Where's the world's most wonderful baby? I'll have to get over to see him again soon."

"Yes, you must," Kaye murmured. "He's growing up in a hurry."

Clancey's head had started to spin like an off-balance top. Kaye had said he was taking care of the baby—showing him off to clients, wasn't that the way she'd phrased it? Had he managed to misplace the child? But wait. If he hadn't even seen the baby lately—

Then she remembered. *Which McKenna,* Hank Gleason had asked suspiciously over lunch the day they'd discussed lawsuits and injunctions. Clancey hadn't paid any attention to the implications of the question then. She'd only been interested in finding out something—anything—about Rowan. She hadn't even registered the fact that there might be another man who carried the name. It hadn't been important.

And it wasn't important now, either, except that it was nice to have the confusion cleared up before she made a fool of herself. At least she didn't have to feel guilty anymore about throwing herself in his arms. That was a great relief.

"About the Christmas tour," Kaye said.

Clancey blinked and tried to pull herself together. Rowan had vanished into the adjacent bedroom; she could hear him whistling.

"If you change your mind, Clancey, just call me. Even if it's the last minute. We really need new places, or people will get tired of the tour and stop coming back. Besides, it's lots of fun."

From Clancey's bedroom came the sound of ripping plaster followed by a voice. "She's only saying that because she's in charge of getting new guinea pigs, Clancey."

Kaye smiled. "Well—perhaps there is some truth to that," she conceded. "But it's not so much work, really. My house has been on the tour for years, in all phases of restoration, and—"

The voice added, "It only seems like years, Kaye."

Kaye looked heavenward and said, very clearly, "Personally, I think Rowan only bought this house because ours is done, and he couldn't stand losing the outlet for all his destructive instincts."

Rowan's head appeared around the corner of the door, his hair and eyebrows liberally coated with white dust. "Just when did you turn into Sigmund Freud, my dear?"

Kaye sighed. "When I first got married, I actually thought it was a bonus to acquire a whole family of brothers," she mused. "Foolish me."

"A whole—how many are there?" Clancey asked tentatively.

"There are four of them," Kaye said darkly. "Now, of course, I wonder how their sister managed to grow up sane."

"Who says she did?" asked the voice from the bedroom.

Kaye stood. "You'll have to come visit me, Clancey. We obviously can't talk seriously this afternoon with him around." She jerked her head toward the door.

As they went downstairs, Clancey couldn't help noticing how the soft autumn sunlight crept through the beveled glass, highlighting the swirling dust particles. It felt as if she was caught in one of the paperweights that created a snowstorm when it was shaken. It would have been fun, except that she knew these tiny particles would creep into every toy and have to be wiped off every box and shelf.

She wasn't aware of sighing until Kaye gave her a sympathetic smile.

"It's not so bad, really," Kaye said. "Of course it would have helped if you'd been able to seal that room off and confine the dust, but these things happen. It's called the mushroom factor, you know—every project, even a small one, mushrooms until it takes in the entire house. Once you've been through it a few times, you learn to expect it."

Clancey smiled a little in return. This was obviously the voice of experience. She wondered if that philosophy was what was keeping Rowan whistling as he worked.

The mushroom factor seemed to be operating in her entire life these days, she found herself thinking after Kaye left. Everything had gone out of control, and no matter what she tried she didn't seem to be able to get things back in hand. Even her silly attempt to discourage Kaye from wanting the house had gone out of whack, just another ill-fated project.

Thank heaven things had turned out as they had. It would take a lot more than a fallen ceiling to discourage Kaye McKenna, that was sure. Rowan was a pushover, in comparison.

Clancey wondered if he was beginning to feel the same way she was—that the house was taking over his life. He might be able to logically explain the collapse of the ceiling, but he certainly hadn't anticipated it. And despite his cheerful whistle a few minutes ago as he attacked the mess, he couldn't be wholeheartedly enjoying the situation, either.

She felt some sympathy for Rowan, when she stopped to think about it. He seemed to be getting stuck with the work, without any of the rewards. She wondered if his enthusiasm for the whole project might be beginning to wear thin. If it was...

She thought about it for a long time, and came to two conclusions: first, that Rowan wouldn't give up on anything as long as he felt that to do so would be admitting defeat, and second, that no matter what was going on in his mind just now, being pleasant to him certainly couldn't hurt her cause. And it just might help.

SHE BAKED ANOTHER PAN of cookies, making sure that they were browned just right on the edges but were still ever-so-slightly chewy in the center. Then she took a plateful and a fresh pot of tea upstairs and placed them safely on the table in the landing.

The bedroom door was closed. At least he was trying to cut down on the mess that filtered into the rest of the house, she thought. That was nice of him.

There was no answer when she knocked, so she pushed the door open cautiously, fearful of tripping over him if he happened to be right inside. But Rowan was in the far corner of the room. He looked over his shoulder, obviously surprised to see her.

He was wearing a filtration mask over his nose and mouth, and powdery grayish white dust had caked his hair and eyebrows and coated his skin with an unnatural pallor.

"That's a great Halloween costume," Clancey said. "You're an octogenarian in an oxygen mask, right? All you need is a little plastic tubing and a hospital gown to complete the effect."

Rowan grunted. "And by the time I finish with this job, I'll walk like I'm eighty, too." He put a hand to the small of his back as if it ached.

"You're a natural," Clancey murmured. "I brought you a snack. I thought you might like a break."

His expression softened—or at least, Clancey thought it did. Under the threateningly bushy gray eyebrows, it was hard to tell.

"Great. I'm almost done, though. Can it wait a couple of minutes?"

She shrugged. "If you want cold cookies, it can wait." She stood in the doorway watching as he pried at the last remaining chunk of ceiling. It resisted, and finally she said, "If it's stuck fast, why does it have to come down?"

"Because it isn't practical to replaster the ceiling, and the modern stuff comes in neat rectangles and won't fit against this raw edge." His voice was slightly muffled by the mask and breathless from the exertion.

Clancey studied the beams that spanned the space above her head. Her eyes were beginning to sting from the particles in the air. "How about opening the windows and letting the dust blow out?" she asked. "Or would that hurt the fresh paint outside?"

Rowan shook his head. "No, but I can't get the windows open."

"Oh, I'd forgotten. Every window I've tried in the whole house has been painted shut."

He groaned. "Just the kind of news I like to hear. With no air conditioning, how did Leonard's tenants stand it in the summer?"

Clancey let it pass. How Rowan coped with the heat next summer would certainly be no problem of hers. "You know, I always wanted a beamed ceiling," she mused.

"Not this kind. It was never intended to be seen."

"Yes, I gathered that." She craned her neck to look at the age-darkened timbers. "How strange, from here it looks as if the boards aren't even straight."

"Oh, they aren't," Rowan said grimly. "They also aren't level, which means the plaster was half an inch thick in some spots and almost two inches in others. The sheer weight helped drag it down. It's going to be loads of fun to replace this." His frustration seemed to lend him strength, and the last stubborn corner came loose with an alarming crack.

Clancey shuddered at the sound of pieces raining down onto the hardwood floor. It was too bad no one had thought of putting down a tarp. Not that it would have made much difference in the long run, she supposed; if the roof itself had collapsed, it couldn't have made much more of a mess.

Rowan went off to wash up, and Clancey found a broom and began sweeping the debris into piles. It took time and care, or a cloud of dust would swirl up and settle into yet another layer on every surface and in every crack. In fact, odd as it was, she didn't even have to be sweeping for it to move around.

It took a few minutes before she realized that there was a definite draft in the front of the room, and longer to find the source of it under the discolored old shade on the front window. She'd raised the shade and was poking at the double-hung sash with Rowan's pry bar when he came back in.

"The worst part of plaster dust is that when you get it wet it turns into concrete," he was saying.

Clancey glanced over her shoulder. His clothes still carried the unnatural grayish cast, but his hair was dark again. It was wet, too—it looked as if he had simply thrust his head under the faucet and let the water sluice over him.

"Look," she said. "Not all the windows were painted shut, after all. This one was painted open half an inch."

He came across to look at it. "That should be a nice source of fresh air all winter."

"Particularly in January, when the arctic wind starts to howl through the gap." She jabbed at the casing again. "And you're the one who's trying to sleep here."

"You really know how to make a point, Clancey," he complained. "Here, let me try."

He seized the upper sash and gave a tremendous tug. At the same instant the pry bar Clancey was wielding broke through the last of the paint that was holding it fast. Clancey could do nothing but watch, eyes wide, unable even to shout a warning, as the sash slammed into place, trapping Rowan's fingers between it and the wood casing.

And she wondered if the little crackling sounds she heard were from the window—or from Rowan's bones snapping under the strain.

CHAPTER SIX

HE DIDN'T BLAST HER with a stream of bad language. Clancey gave him credit for that. Even though she had to pry open the lower sash and reach under it in order to tug the top one down so she could free his fingers, all Rowan did was moan. Clancey herself was shuddering at the pain that must be echoing through him with each vibration of the window. But finally he could pull free.

He could not, however, straighten his fingers from the clawlike position in which they'd been caught. Even the effort brought tiny beads of sweat to his upper lip and a pallor that rivaled the dusty look he'd had earlier.

"Ice," she said briefly, and ran for the refrigerator.

Rowan followed her downstairs very slowly and watched as she began dumping ice-cube trays into the nearest container. It happened to be the dishpan, and when she gestured to him to put his hands atop the heaped ice, he protested. "What are you trying to do, give me frostbite, too?"

"At least then you'd be too numb to feel the pain on the way to the hospital. For any injury of this sort, the first treatment is ice." Then she ruined the professional sound of that by adding, "Isn't it?"

He rolled his eyes and cooperated. Clancey swathed a towel around his hands and started dumping another layer of cubes over them, as gently as she could.

Rowan winced as an ice cube bounced off his knuckle, and said plaintively, "Why stop with my hands? Why not just put me on the first train to Siberia and freeze my feet, too?"

Clancey relaxed a little. If he was starting with the wisecracks again, he was going to be all right.

CLANCEY STOPPED THE CAR by the emergency entrance and came around to help Rowan get out. He paused just inside the emergency-room door. "You can't leave the car there. It's double-parked."

"I know. I'll move it as soon as they start working on you."

"Are you kidding? They won't even touch my wounds till all the insurance forms are out of the way." Then he groaned in what sounded like mortal agony.

"It's getting worse, isn't it?" she asked. Guilt welled up in her so strongly she was almost physically sick herself.

"It's not my hands, exactly. It's the thought of all the paperwork."

"Oh, I see what you mean. Well, maybe they'll let you make an *X* instead of signing your name."

"Not only that," he muttered. "There's the problem of my insurance identification card."

"Don't tell me you don't have it."

"Well, I wasn't expecting to have an accident," he began.

"Nobody ever does, Rowan! That's included in the damned definition of the word!"

"Would you hush? I do have the card. It's in my wallet."

Clancey glared at him. "Then what's the problem?"

"The wallet is in my hip pocket."

And if he couldn't move his fingers he wasn't going to be reaching into the back pocket of those formfitting jeans, either. Someone else was going to have to retrieve his wallet.

Clancey sighed. "Turn around." She slid her fingers into his pocket. The leather wallet was warm and supple from the heat of his body, and unexpectedly slick. On her first try it slipped out of her grip, and she had to dig deeper, till almost her whole hand was out of sight. That wasn't the worst of it, however; the blue denim was so soft and well-worn it was practically nonexistent. Clancey could feel herself turning red.

Rowan was looking over his shoulder. "I wouldn't recommend a second career as a pickpocket if you can't do any better than that, Clancey."

She got hold of a corner of the wallet and yanked it out. She felt like slapping it into his palm. Instead she settled for handing it over to the clerk who had come to greet them, and without another word went to move the car.

It would serve Rowan right if she just drove off and left him there.

On the other hand, it had been her window, and she'd been pushing on it when his fingers got in the way, so she did have a responsibility to see him through this. And if it turned out that all his fingers were broken . . .

Well, she could always buy him that ticket to Siberia, she decided bleakly. It would be a whole lot easier than listening to him, that was sure.

When she returned to the emergency room the clerk showed her down the hall to the treatment cubicle where a nurse was bending over Rowan. "Are your hands normally this cold?" she was asking as Clancey came in.

Rowan sent an I-told-you-so look at Clancey over the nurse's shoulder. "No, that was the half ton of ice she packed me in."

"Oh. Well, icing it down was a good idea, actually."

Clancey stuck her tongue out at Rowan.

"It's a good thing you weren't wearing a wedding ring, Mr. McKenna," the nurse went on. "Your finger's so swollen, we would've had to cut the ring off. I'll get you over to radiology in a minute for your X rays. Just sit still now."

She smiled and whisked out of the room.

Clancey perched on the edge of a chair. "What gave her the idea you *have* a wedding ring?"

He shrugged. "Simple logic, I suppose."

"Just because I'm here to hold your hand?"

He jerked back a little, protective of the injured fingers.

"Figuratively speaking, of course. I'm not about to touch you again."

"Thank heaven," Rowan said piously.

"Why did you want me, anyway? The clerk said you asked her to bring me in."

"Look, Clancey, I'm damned if I'm going to explain all by myself how this happened."

"Thanks. I suppose it's better to defend myself. Otherwise you'll make it sound like I did it on purpose."

Rowan nodded. "Assault with a deadly window, I think they call it."

In the end, the X rays showed that nothing was broken. "You're very lucky," the doctor concluded as he wrapped the last injured knuckle. "The force was distributed equally across all your fingers, so none of them took the full brunt of the blow."

Rowan's expression was incredulous as he looked down at his bandaged hands. Only his thumbs and his pinkies had escaped. "This is lucky?" he said, almost hoarsely.

Clancey got him out of there as quickly as she could, before he became hysterical.

As SOON AS THE CAR stopped in the driveway Rowan automatically reached for the door handle and muttered something under his breath when the bulky supports and bandages got in the way. "If nothing's broken," he went on more loudly, "then why all the splints?"

"To keep you from hurting yourself more."

"Well, that's one sure way to prevent it—make sure I can't do anything. It's going to be nearly impossible to drive."

"Drive?" Clancey's voice was no more than a squeak. "You can't mean you're planning to drive yourself home?"

"How else do you suggest I get there? My apartment is clear across town."

"I'll take you."

"And leave my car here?"

Clancey shrugged. "No doubt I could drive it."

"Great. And then you'd be stuck at my place without a way to get back."

The way he said it, Clancey thought, indicated that the idea of having her around seemed to him more of a handicap than all six bandaged fingers put together. She didn't blame him, exactly, so she tried another approach. "The label on the painkiller bottle says you shouldn't drive while you're taking it. And you've had two of them—remember?"

He didn't answer.

So it wasn't that he didn't possess common sense; he just didn't want to exercise it at the moment. "Look," Clancey said. "Let's say for the sake of argument that you manage to get yourself home without cracking up your car. Do you live alone?"

He nodded.

"Then how do you plan to unlock the door? And what do you plan to eat?"

"I'm not hungry."

"You will be once the shock wears off. And you're not in any shape to use even a can opener, Rowan."

He glowered at her.

Clancey was beginning to regret that she'd found out he wasn't married. *I could have turned him over to Kaye without a qualm.*

"I'm already feeling like a worm, you know. At least let me help, would you? I cook a mean—" she paused, wondering what on earth he might be able to eat, and went on hopefully "—stir-fry, and as soon as you have something to eat I'll drive you home and take a cab back."

He showed no sign of having heard her.

Clancey lost her temper. "And don't get the idea that I'm trying to hold you hostage because of your wonderful temperament, McKenna! I'd be glad to see the last of you, but I'll feel awful if you have a wreck on top of everything else, so I am not going to let you out of my car as long as you're threatening to drive yours. And you can't open the door by yourself, can you? Or you wouldn't be sitting here listening to me. That's it. If you don't cooperate, you're just going to have to stay out here all night."

"So there," he said under his breath.

Clancey folded her arms and glared at him.

He added innocently, "I was just finishing up the lecture for you, since you were obviously running out of breath. All right. I'll cooperate. Now will you let me out of this tin prison you call a car?"

"What's wrong with my car?" Clancey seized the change of subject. At least he was talking.

"It's one of the six worst models on the road at surviving a collision, that's what," he said as she helped him get out. He followed her up the front walk. "Hit a road sign at twenty and it's totaled. The car, not the road sign. Hit a truck and it's good-night, sweet princess—"

"Thank you." Clancey dug her house key out and ushered him through the front door.

He was frowning suspiciously. "For what?"

She rewarded him with a soft smile. "For caring whether I'm safe on the highway," she murmured. "I think you'll be most comfortable in my living room upstairs. Are you feeling steady enough to make it by yourself, or do you need a hand?"

"It's my fingers that got hurt, Clancey—not my toes. I can walk."

She refused to take offense. "Then I'll get you something to drink while I fix dinner. What would you like?"

"Coffee."

She looked a little doubtful, but he had already dragged himself up to the first landing by then, so she didn't argue.

When she took up his coffee a few minutes later, Rowan was sitting on the couch with his eyes closed and his head lolling against the high back. His legs sprawled across the carpet and his hands rested awkwardly with the palms up, one on each thigh. He looked miserable.

The drawn look touched her heart, and she almost put her hand out to smooth his hair back from his temple, but she stopped herself at the last minute. She brought over a small table instead and set it beside him to hold his coffee.

He opened his eyes then. "That smells good." He reached for the cup, curling his little finger into the handle and bracing his thumb against the side, but despite his care the cup started to tip uncontrollably. "Dammit!"

Clancey caught it and guided it over to the table.

Rowan let his head fall back against the couch. "Thank you. I thought I was headed to the emergency room again—with burns this time."

"I was expecting that. I tried it out with an empty cup downstairs, you see, and I didn't have any success."

His eyes opened to wary slits. "So you brought it up to see whether I'd make a fool of myself? How entertaining for you."

"Not at all. I thought perhaps you'd be more dexterous than I was. But just in case—" She pulled her hand out from behind her back. "I also brought this."

He eyed it with something close to malevolence. "A curlicue straw. How thoughtful."

Clancey held it up for closer inspection. It was a garishly colored thing, nearly a yard long if it had been straight, and a good many of the twists and curves were enclosed in a clear plastic bubble shaped like a turtle's shell. "Straight out of Small World's inventory," she added. "I've sold hundreds of these things. The kids love them, because it looks like everything you drink is filtered through the turtle's digestive system before it reaches your mouth."

"I can see that. Thank you for trying to cheer me up with this thoughtful gift, Clancey, but—"

"Well, I don't seem to have any ordinary straws. If you'd rather, I can pour the coffee into a glass. I think you might manage that better. Except the glass would get awfully hot."

"Oh, leave the straw," he said with disgust. "I'll drink with my eyes closed."

Clancey tried to hide her smile. "What kind of little boy were you, anyway, if you didn't get enthused about frogs and turtles and things like that?"

"Well, I never had a particular fascination with their insides. I suppose you did?"

"Hated them. I almost flunked biology because we had to dissect frogs. I couldn't even learn to fish because I couldn't stand the smell of worms—"

"It breaks my heart to interrupt this fascinating reminiscence, but I don't suppose you know if there's anything fit to watch on television at the moment?"

"Not offhand." She poked through the basket beside her favorite chair and handed him the remote control, then watched in dismay as he stabbed ineffectually at the tiny buttons with his thumb. She took the gadget back and turned the television on. "Football? News? Opera?"

"Anything will do, as long as it's not a documentary about turtles, frogs or worms." He wasn't watching, anyway; he'd let his head fall back against the couch cushions again.

Clancey smiled a little. At least his mind wasn't completely on his fingers anymore.

When she brought dinner in a little later, he'd managed to change the channel, and a promotion was airing for a television movie. "Oh, I want to see that one," Clancey said as she arranged a plate on the small table for him. "When does it come on?"

"Ten minutes. You have perfect timing." He eyed the steaming plate of chicken, rice and vegetables with a mixture of hunger and apprehension, then sighed and balanced a fork between thumb and pinkie finger and stabbed a bite-sized chunk.

It was slow going, but he managed.

Clancey watched in sympathy. "You aren't going to be lifting weights for a while, are you?" she murmured, and pulled her chair around at a more comfortable angle.

The movie was well under way when he laid his fork down with a sigh.

"Finished?" Clancey asked.

He nodded. "That was good. And you were right. I was hungrier than I thought. If you're anxious to get rid of me..."

"As a matter of fact, I'd rather not miss the end of the movie. I just wondered if you were ready for dessert." She dug around in the basket beside her chair and came up with a candy bar. "Gourmet chocolate, from my secret stash."

"Sounds good. But I don't think I can unwrap it."

Clancey moved over to the couch. She broke off a corner of the bar and put it on his tongue. Indistinctly, Rowan said, "I'm pretty useless, aren't I?" His hands lay palm up in his lap, motionless, as if it hurt to move them at all.

Perhaps I should have fed him, Clancey thought, just to save him the effort. "Oh, not useless, exactly," she said lightly. "Just think. If I was into needlepoint, you could hold the skeins of yarn on your splints while I rewound them into balls. That's an important contribution to society. Or—"

He made a face, and she giggled and put another chunk of chocolate into his mouth. He captured her fingertip as well, and worried it lightly between his teeth for a moment.

"Hey," Clancey protested, "that's not edible!"

The tip of his tongue fluttered against her nail and then slowly began to sample the soft pad at the end of her finger. The sensation was incredible—something like the tiny pinpricks when blood circulation came back after a period of being cut off, but magnified a hundredfold. And it prickled not only through her finger, but shot up her arm and surged through her entire body....

It took a tremendous effort of will for Clancey to tug her fingertip away. Not because Rowan was holding it so tightly, for he wasn't. The grip of his teeth had never been more than teasing. It was because something inside her didn't want to sever that tenuous connection.

Her hand was trembling a little as she broke off another piece of chocolate. This had to stop, she warned herself, and looked up at him very deliberately, intending to show she was completely unmoved by his antics.

The mischievous look died out of his eyes as she watched, and the quirky smile vanished from the corner of his mouth. He had a beautiful mouth, she thought. It was shaped just right.

He leaned forward a little and paused, just looking at her. That much again, and his lips would touch hers. Yes, he did have a beautiful mouth, not thick lipped, not thin. And that smile... But of course, he wasn't smiling at the moment; he was—

The telephone shrilled from the landing. Rowan jumped as if a siren had gone off in his ear, and Clancey put the candy bar hastily down and went to answer it, caught somewhere between irritation and relief at the interruption.

Eileen said, "Sorry to bother you, Clancey. But Hank phoned while you were out for lunch today, and I was so busy I forgot to write it down. He wanted you to call him back."

"Hank?"

"Yes," Eileen said impatiently. "You know, the faithful attorney who's never in his life been called Hank the Hunk. What's wrong with you tonight? Or is it bad timing? Did I interrupt a wrestling match on the couch?"

"Not at all."

"I didn't think it was likely."

"Don't gloat. How was your date with the mad driver from the supermarket?"

"Must you rub it in, Clancey?" There was a shiver in Eileen's voice. "There would be a real demand for a gigolo service in this town. Somebody could make millions."

"You, I suppose?" Clancey sounded amused.

"Don't say it, I know what you're thinking. Not if I can't even find a man for myself. I'll have to work on it."

Clancey put the telephone down and went back to the living room. She was enjoying the movie much more than she would a chat with Hank, she told herself, and smothered the tiny twinge of conscience that said her enjoyment had nothing to do with the movie.

Besides, the call must be about her lease. She'd dropped off a copy at Hank's office last week. And she could hardly talk to him about that with Rowan in the next room, could she?

Rowan's feet were still on the floor, but the rest of him had crashed into a horizontal position. As she stood there looking down at him, he snuggled his cheek farther into the pillow she'd used last night.

"Great," she muttered. "Still in his clothes, and still here. So much for taking him home." She lifted his feet onto the couch, and he flung out a hand and uttered a pained moan in his sleep.

Well, perhaps it was better this way, Clancey decided. At least he wouldn't wake up alone, needing something and with no way to get it. After all, the poor man couldn't even get the top off the painkiller bottle without help.

He didn't stir when she covered him with a blanket. He was more than just asleep, she thought; he was

GET 4 BOOKS

FREE

Return this card, and we'll send you 4 brand-new Harlequin Romance® novels, absolutely *FREE!* We'll even pay the postage both ways!

We're making you this offer to introduce you to the benefits of the Harlequin Reader Service®: free home delivery of brand-new romance novels, months before they're available in stores, **AND** at a saving of 40¢ apiece compared to the cover price!

Accepting these 4 free books places you under no obligation to continue. You may cancel at any time, even just after receiving your free shipment. If you do not cancel, every month we'll send 6 more Harlequin Romance novels and bill you just $2.49* apiece—that's all!

Yes! Please send me my 4 free Harlequin Romance novels, as explained above.

Name

Address   Apt.

City   State   Zip

116 CIH AGNR (U-H-R-11/92)

Get 4 Books FREE

SEE BACK OF CARD FOR DETAILS

FREE MYSTERY GIFT

We will be happy to send you a free bonus gift along with your free books! To request it, please check here and mail this reply card promptly!

Thank you!

BUSINESS REPLY CARD

FIRST CLASS MAIL   PERMIT NO. 717   BUFFALO, NY

POSTAGE WILL BE PAID BY ADDRESSEE

HARLEQUIN READER SERVICE®
3010 WALDEN AVE
P O BOX 1867
BUFFALO NY 14240-9952

DETACH ALONG DOTTED LINE AND MAIL TODAY! – DETACH ALONG DOTTED LINE AND MAIL TODAY! – DETACH ALONG DOTTED LINE AND MAIL TODAY! – DETACH ALONG DOTTED LINE AND MAIL TODAY!

practically unconscious. He must have been holding himself upright through sheer willpower.

It was just as well that kiss had come to nothing. It was obvious the pain relievers had been kicking in just about then, and so he was hardly responsible for his actions.

And the landlord kissing the tenant would have been a complication neither of them needed. Or wanted, she reminded herself.

ROWAN HAD ROUSED a couple of times in the night for a drink of water, but he'd been so groggy from the effect of the painkillers that Clancey wasn't quite sure he'd even realized where he was. Toward morning, though, he fell into a sounder sleep, and by the time she got up for the day he was still out like a light.

She took a shower, letting the hot water pour over her neck, stiff from yet another night on the floor. "I'm getting too old for this," she muttered as she tugged on a silky cream-colored sweater and heather tweed slacks and went back to the living room.

What on earth was she to do with the man on her couch?

She stared down at him and debated the question. Even rumpled and displaying a definite morning-after stubble of beard he didn't look bad; still he was no sleeping beauty. Well, that eliminated one possible move; she wasn't going to kiss him awake.

Somewhere there was an accounting firm that would be expecting him to come to work. Not that he'd be much use today, she was positive of that. Still, someone would need to know he wasn't coming in, and if Rowan himself didn't wake up soon, she supposed it would be up to her.

Eileen was already in the shop, with the money in the cash drawer, the lights on and the door open for business. She gave Clancey an appraising glance. "You look terrible. Are you certain you want to stick to the story that there was no wrestling match on the couch last night?"

"No. I mean, yes, I want to stick to my story."

Eileen nodded wisely. "It happened on the floor, then?"

Clancey ignored her and reached for the telephone book. She found Rowan in the small print under Accountants, listed by just his name and a street address she vaguely recognized as being in the center of the professional district downtown.

She was dialing the telephone when Eileen said, "Dear heaven, what happened to you?"

The fascinated horror in the woman's voice was its own explanation; Clancey needed no other warning. She turned around just as Rowan reached the bottom step. "Good," she said. "I was just calling you in sick. I didn't know what else to do."

Rowan shrugged. "Go ahead. I sure don't plan to go to work, and I'm certain everybody in the office would enjoy hearing your explanation."

He was still pale, she thought, and rather weak. And very rumpled, after a night in his clothes. And with that dark stubble on his cheeks...

He looked wonderful, she concluded. It was something about the eyes. With those intense dark blue eyes fixed on her, everything else faded into obscurity.

"I wasn't planning to explain, exactly," she said. "I just didn't want you to get in trouble with the boss for not even calling, so—"

The receiver clicked in her hand. "Martin and McKenna. This is Jean. May I help you?" said a soft voice in her ear.

He wasn't an employee; he was a partner. Clancey supposed she should have anticipated that. She thrust the telephone at him.

Rowan grimaced and caught it between ear and shoulder. "I won't be in today, Jean. What? No, nothing so pleasant. I was attacked by a vengeful window."

Eileen's eyes rounded.

"No, not widow," he said patiently, "*window*. It slammed on my fingers."

"Isn't that just our luck?" Eileen asked under her breath. "The only good-looking guy who hangs around the neighborhood turns out to be a Peeping Tom." Clancey glared at her, and Eileen asked practically, "Well? What other kind of man gets a window slammed on his hands?"

Clancey retrieved the telephone from its precarious perch and hung it up. "Shall I drive you home?"

Rowan shook his head. "No. You're busy, and I've got a little more flexibility this morning. I can manage."

"But—"

"I won't take any pain pills till I get home, all right? But you could start the car for me, Clancey. I'm not sure I can manage that bit."

She didn't argue about it. It was apparent that he couldn't wait to get away—from the house, or from her, or both. And she certainly wasn't going to beg him to stay. The last thing she wanted was to look as if she was turning into some sort of fool over Rowan McKenna!

Besides, he was clear-eyed this morning, and obviously in control of himself, so she didn't argue. She helped him put on his coat and walked out to the street with him, unlocked his car and started the engine.

When it was running smoothly she stepped back out, and found to her surprise that he had moved just a little and was blocking the open door. His wrists were propped on the car roof so that his arms formed a sort of fence over her shoulders. She could retreat into the driver's seat or she could stand there. Of course, she could step on his toes. She had no doubt he'd move quickly enough, with that threat looming.

But before she could make up her mind, he said, "I didn't thank you last night for taking care of me when I didn't even realize I needed taking care of." His voice was ever-so-slightly husky.

She shrugged uncomfortably. "Anyone would have done it."

"No, most people would have given up and let me be stubborn even if it killed me. Thank you, Clancey."

There was something in his voice that almost frightened her. She looked up just as he bent his head, and saw that his eyes had gone very dark.

He didn't even have to be touching her, Clancey discovered, to send those prickles of anticipation racing through her. Prickles that stung and ached and paralyzed—

The truth was, she didn't want to move away. She swallowed hard and her gaze dropped to that beautifully shaped mouth of his, and her own lips softened and parted just a little.

"I hope you don't mind," he whispered, "but shaving was out of the question this morning."

His lips touched hers softly, moving gently, clinging and caressing, until Clancey's head was swimming and the blood was pounding in her ears, and rational thinking was only something vaguely remembered from long ago. When he released her she managed to say, in a sort of croak, "I don't mind," and only when she saw the green light of mischief rekindle in his eyes did she realize what an invitation it had been.

"I'll remember that," he promised, and stepped back to let her go.

Clancey fled toward the house. Rowan stood there for a moment longer, rubbing the back of his wrist thoughtfully against his stubbly chin, and then he drove away.

His lips touched hers softly and lingeringly, clinging to a caressing, until Clancey's head was swimming and the blood was rushing to her ears, and she realized dimly it was only something vaguely remembered from long ago. When he kissed her she managed to say, a sort of croak... only a whisper, when she saw the green light of another blonde... to his eyes old she...somewhat in a vision it had been

CHAPTER SEVEN

SHE BURST INTO THE HOUSE and then deliberately slowed her pace and her breathing. If she didn't get control of herself, she might as well take out an ad in the newspaper saying Rowan McKenna had kissed her, and she liked it.

And as for practically asking him to do it again—what an idiot she was. It had been a single, well-meant thank-you kiss, that was all. There was certainly nothing about it to cause heart palpitations; no wonder he'd been amused by her reaction. Maybe, if she was lucky, he wouldn't come around anymore. That would solve several of her problems. In the meantime she was just glad there hadn't been a hundred customers standing there to see her make a fool of herself.

But of course, there was Eileen. "All right, what gives?" she demanded the moment Clancey came back into sight. "At first I thought you whacked him for trying something, though I couldn't imagine why you let him spend the night after that. Or perhaps the night together came first, and he did something to offend you this morning."

"Eileen—"

The stream of speculation was not to be stopped. "But then how did his fingers get so neatly bandaged? If you were the cause of the injury, you must have had a reason, and I can't imagine you turning around and playing Florence Nightingale to fix him up."

"Eileen, it's none of your business!"

"On the other hand, the way you called in sick for him certainly sounded as if you planned to take the day off and play house. And kissing him goodbye in the driveway like that—"

"I ought to have known you'd be watching," Clancey groaned. "Do you always stare out the window?"

"Only when there aren't any customers to attend to."

"Then I'll try to scare some up to keep you busy," Clancey muttered and retreated to the stockroom, ostensibly to plot her advertising for the next few weeks.

And, although Rowan's face kept intruding at odd intervals, the amazing thing was that she managed to keep her mind pretty much on business.

The trick was going to be balancing her prices just right in order to maximize both sales and profits through Christmas. That way she could cut down the sheer volume to be moved in January, and still have money enough to get herself reestablished. It wouldn't be easy, with the increased inventory she'd ordered when she leased the house....

Clancey closed her eyes in pain at the mere prospect of starting all over again. Sometimes she just wanted to crawl into the nearest closet and cry.

But that was a quitter's attitude, and Clancey reminded herself briskly that she wasn't a quitter. If she was, she'd have given up the idea of a store during her first year in business, and gone back to working for someone else. But she had survived those first lean years, and she would survive this, too. It was a bad roll of the dice, that was all. She'd just have to make the best of it.

She straightened her shoulders and started work in earnest. She had loads of fashion dolls on hand, and boxes of clothes for them; she could take a twenty-percent markdown on those, and advertise the sale. A few big, well-placed ads should bring in lots of people who would want other things as well....

She was so involved that when the telephone rang she scarcely heard it.

"I thought you'd have called me back by now," Hank said, sounding a little irritable, when she finally answered.

Clancey crossed her fingers. "I just got your message." It wasn't such a very big fib, after all, and the way Eileen had been acting lately, she deserved to have her reputation maligned. "You've had a chance to look at the lease, then?"

"Yes. It's only an ordinary lease. I can't find any reason for you not to sign it."

"Thanks, Hank—"

He hadn't even paused. "The problem is, if it's so ordinary, why does he need it? You already had a perfectly good lease."

My very thought, Clancey told herself. There was something wrong somewhere. But she said reasonably, "The old one was for three years, that's why. He wants out of it lots sooner than that."

"He could have just amended it. There's something distinctly odd about this, I'm convinced of it. Are you certain McKenna wants to live there? It's not his kind of neighborhood. He might just be going into the slum landlord business, you know."

"Then why would he want to get rid of me?"

"Because you're the kind of tenant who will make a fuss if things aren't right. Most businesses are. People who rent ordinary apartments in that sort of location, on the other hand, don't—''

Clancey interrupted. "Slum lords don't paint the place and put a new roof on it."

She could almost hear Hank chewing on that one. "Not usually," he admitted. "Look, I've got to run. My client's waiting. We'll talk about this Saturday night at the civic center dinner."

Clancey groaned a little.

"You hadn't forgotten, had you? The tickets cost the earth. We've got to go."

I wish I could just forget, she thought.

The frantic pace of the three-day grand opening had given way to a more settled, flexible routine, but the idea of a formal dinner on one of her rare nights off was less than exciting. Still, it was for a good cause, she reminded herself. The town desperately needed that new civic center, and if a few fund-raisers could convince the city fathers to move the project along, Clancey could bear to put on a formal dress and smile at all of Hank's friends for an evening. There might be somebody interesting in the crowd.

It reminded her of her mostly tongue-in-cheek advice to Eileen. A woman didn't meet eligible men by staying at home. Perhaps that's what was wrong with her; she'd been keeping too busy lately. No wonder Rowan McKenna seemed so appealing. It wasn't anything personal. She'd probably have had much the same reaction to any man in similar circumstances.

And the very next time she saw him, Clancey decided, she would make that perfectly clear to him, too. There was no sense in letting him go around thinking she found him irresistible, or something.

BUT IN FACT, CLANCEY didn't see him for days. At first it was a relief to be able to get on with life without Rowan's interference, but when the third full day went by without him popping in, his absence began to annoy her just as much as his presence had. Did he seriously think she was so infatuated with him that he had to keep his distance?

Or was there something else altogether? Despite Clancey's best intentions, Hank's words had taken root in her mind. She studied every line of that simple little lease, backward and forward, feeling like an idiot all the while. If Hank had been unable to find anything less than straightforward, how could she expect to unravel it? Still, she couldn't shake the conviction that there was something wrong with the lease.

And then as the days dragged by and the weather turned chilly and the roofers didn't show up, she began to wonder if Hank's wildest suspicions might be right after all—that Rowan just wanted her to move so he could rent the apartments to less-discerning tenants.

Had Rowan ever actually said he wanted to live in the house? Or had he simply allowed Clancey to infer it, based on her own love of the place? She honestly couldn't remember. In any case, could she put faith in whatever he might have said? He wasn't exactly accountable to her.

A slum lord wouldn't paint the house and put a new roof on it, she'd told Hank rather loftily. But, on the other hand, what had actually been done to the house since Rowan had become its owner?

She ticked the items off on her fingers. Most of the old siding had a fresh coat of paint, a few shingles had been stripped off the porch roof, one of the ceilings was gone and the front window in her bedroom now closed nice and tight. That was about the size of the changes— it made no sense to call them all "improvements."

And Rowan's investment had been minimal. She wasn't sure how much the back taxes had amounted to, but certainly less than the cost of a house on the open market. And the paint job had cost no more than the price of supplies and food for his volunteer labor. As for the roof repair—well, so far it seemed to be imaginary. And for all she knew, by now the locksmith had turned his bill over to a collection agency for lack of payment....

Stop being crazy, she told herself. The man had six crushed fingers; she could hardly blame him for not climbing around on ladders and scaffolds to finish up the painting. And since she'd been the cause of the crushed fingers, she couldn't really blame him for avoiding her, at least till he healed. Or perhaps things weren't healing right. Perhaps he wasn't able to do anything at all. Perhaps he'd gotten an infection and they might have to amputate—

She thought that one over for half of Friday morning, and left quite a lot of tooth marks in a perfectly good pencil. She hadn't even sent him a get-well card, she reflected.

She reached out to finger the flowers he'd sent her last week. The petals were still soft and supple, the colors bright. The helium balloons had lost their oomph, however, and were drooping sadly.

She hadn't thought of sending him a gift, assuming that he'd be back long before now.

"To follow up on that kiss, no doubt," she muttered. "What an idiot you are, Clancey Kincade!"

The receptionist at the accounting firm put her call through without hesitation. It was a good omen, that he was at the office, Clancey told herself. Or was it a bad one, because he obviously wasn't busy?

She didn't have time to think about it before Rowan murmured, "Well, hello, there. Any more hapless men get caught in your windows lately?"

She ignored that, but it took an effort. "I called to see if you're feeling better."

"Somewhat. I still have trouble holding things, but I've discovered that I can punch the keys of the calculator with the eraser end of a pencil, so at least I'm back to work. I'm not up to speed, however. Tax season will be here before I get this fall's work done."

She gulped a little. "I'm so sorry, Rowan."

She heard a crackling sound, like papers shuffling on his desk. "And of course I've been told not to expect to play the violin again."

There was a brief silence in which the world seemed to stagger to a halt. Clancey closed her eyes in pain.

"I had no idea," she whispered. "When...who...?"

"It was my mother who told me to give it up, actually. I was eleven at the time, and the cat kept running away from home whenever I'd practice."

Clancey shrieked, "You rotten, miserable— You were going to let me believe I'd ruined your hands?"

"Please," Rowan protested. "I didn't ask for my eardrum to be pierced."

"You're asking to be boiled in oil! I thought you were serious—that you were planning to turn professional or something!"

"That's what my mother thought, too. At first. It took quite a bit to convince her otherwise. Do you know how long it takes to train a cat to do a trick like that? Especially when the cat doesn't want to learn."

"Rowan, I do not want to hear it." She took a deep breath and said firmly, "I actually had two reasons for calling."

"Oh? Let me guess."

She wasn't about to cooperate with that sort of nonsense. "About the ceiling in my bedroom," she went on, before his speculations could get out of hand. "I wanted to know if you were planning to repair it."

"Of course not," he said easily. It was obvious that he didn't even pause to think it over.

She was almost stunned. He couldn't be planning to leave it that way. He'd said himself that those support beams were never meant to be looked at. But a slum lord just might, she found herself thinking.

"That's an inside job," Rowan went on. "Which makes it strictly your territory."

"So was taking down the old one an inside job," she pointed out.

"Oh, but that was different. It was dangerous then, and if it had fallen and hurt you, you could have sued me."

"Not exactly," she muttered. "You made me promise not to sue, remember?"

"Well, yes, I did, but you know how nit-picking juries can be about that sort of agreement. Now it's safe, so the rest is up to you. Was there anything else you wanted to chat about?"

She had to bite her tongue long and hard, but she managed to say civilly, "You know, I was really only asking if I should expect you to leave another mess for me to clean up."

"Not me," he was saying cheerfully as she hung up on him.

She found herself wondering if it would have changed his attitude any if she'd volunteered to sign that bland little lease.

Then she decided that she'd just as soon not know. In a couple of months it wouldn't be her business what he did.

ON SATURDAY THE WEATHER was gray and gloomy and damp. It was the kind of day that made it painfully clear the last gasp of summer had gone and winter was hovering nearby.

Clancey could feel the cold humidity in her bones. Apparently her customers could, too, for the store was nearly deserted. Only a few die-hard shoppers came in, and they bought little.

As the front door closed behind each one, Clancey shivered in the cutting cold of the draft and told herself stoutly that next week, when her new advertising campaign began in earnest, things would get better.

She was taking advantage of the slow traffic to catch up on some bookkeeping chores when the door opened again, the little warning bell she'd hung above it chiming cheerfully. She looked up with a smile that quickly died as Rowan came in.

He leaned over the counter and put his index finger under her chin. "You look as if you've lost your last teddy bear," he mused.

"I see you're using your fingers again."

He tipped his head to one side appraisingly. "Are you avoiding the subject?" But he didn't pursue it. Instead, he flexed his hands carefully, as if he was still trying out an unfamiliar gadget. "Well, they're all working again, but not consistently. And a couple are still sort of numb. Have you happened to see my paintbrushes?''

She stopped feeling sorry for him; he couldn't be in such awful shape, after all. "In a box on the back porch where you left them. Isn't it a rotten day to paint?''

"One does it when one is able," he pointed out. "And since all week I haven't been able—"

Clancey lost her temper. "Look, Rowan, it was an accident, all right? I didn't hold your hands down and slam the window on purpose, you know. So would you stop trying to make me feel guilty?''

He looked astounded. "Me?" he protested. "I wouldn't dream of such a thing. I was just stating facts."

That was enough to make her feel really silly. She wasn't entirely convinced his comment had been innocent. Still, if he was the sort who held grudges, he had much bigger things to resent than a set of smashed fingers, didn't he?

She looked up at him through her lashes. His eyes were dark and sincere, with not a single glint of mischievous green. Clancey's gaze dropped to her checkbook, lying open on the counter next to the cash register. "Sorry," she said stiffly. "I guess I just feel so bad about it that I expect you to be angry."

Rowan closed his hand into a fist. "Would you feel better if I beat you up?''

Clancey smiled ruefully. "Almost," she admitted.

"All right. I'd say a punch in the jaw equals six bruised fingers." His knuckles tapped her chin softly. "There. Now we're even."

His fingertips slid across her cheek, a gentle caress that almost brought tears to her eyes. She blinked a couple of times, hoping he hadn't seen, and said, "Good. Now I can stop worrying about that and get all my attention back on this blasted checkbook."

Rowan smiled. "What's the matter? It won't balance?"

She gestured at the long strand of paper tape that coiled out of the calculator at her elbow and trailed across the floor. "No, it won't. And I've been working at it for an hour." She bent her head over the book with a frown. Her hair swung forward, blocking her face from view. But that meant she couldn't see him, either, so it was intuition that warned her when he moved around the end of the counter to stand beside her stool.

"Let me see." He gathered up a handful of her hair that was in his way and tucked it behind her ear. His hand came to rest on the nape of her neck, almost absentmindedly.

Clancey tried to stop breathing, because any motion at all, no matter how tiny, turned that simple contact into a warm and sensual massage. At least, it felt that way to her. She was relatively certain that for Rowan it was simply a convenient place to lean, and perhaps a bit of soothing body warmth for his still-sore knuckles. But it wasn't possible to sit there forever without taking in oxygen, and the longer he looked at her neat row of entries the more agitated she became.

What was he doing, anyway, she wondered. He was just looking at the checkbook, not touching the calculator or glancing at the tape she'd run. He didn't even have a pencil in his hand.

He was standing so close to her his shoulder was brushing hers, and the scent of him tingled in her nose. She was trying to figure out what elements of it were soap, which were after-shave, and which were purely Rowan when he tapped a line in the checkbook. "There it is."

Clancey's jaw dropped. "Oh, come on. You can't have done that in your head."

He shrugged. "Give me a half-dozen dollar bills and I'll add up the serial numbers faster than you can run the calculator. I used to win a lot of barroom bets that way."

"I thought you didn't gamble."

"That's not gambling, Clancey. It's a sure thing." He seemed to realize his hand was still nestled against her hair, and slowly removed it.

The sudden chill against the nape of her neck made Clancey want to shiver.

Rowan looked around, seeming to notice the uncharacteristic quiet for the first time. "No Eileen today?"

"She's got a head cold."

"No wonder, with this weather. It's chilly in here. I thought you said the boiler was in great shape."

"The problem is right here—every time the front door opens half the warm air in the house rushes out. Not that I'm complaining," she added hastily.

"That's good. I think you're right about the paint. Maybe I'll just prune some of the bushes and then go home and watch the football game."

"Sometimes I envy people who have weekends off."

"I noticed you seem to work all the time."

She shrugged. "Usually Eileen and I split it up so we get at least one free day a week. And I'd planned to hire another clerk for the Christmas rush, but with the uncertain state of affairs here, I decided it would be better not to spend the money.''

"You'd rather end up exhausted?"

"I'll have plenty of time to rest after Christmas.''

If she expected an outpouring of sympathy, or an offer to let her stay a little longer if it would help, Clancey was doomed to disappointment.

Rowan merely said, "That's true," and went off to search for a pair of pruning shears he swore had been in the garage last time he'd looked.

Clancey cursed under her breath at the cold air he'd let in. It wasn't so bad as long as she was moving around the store, but sitting or standing at the cash register was enough to chill her through. She hated to think what it would be like when the weather really got cold.

"Not my problem," she reminded herself.

She had to hunt through the stockroom to find the tiny electric heater that had kept her toes warm all last winter in the other store. Two customers came in to browse just as she was setting it up, and the blast of damp, chilly air that swirled in with them made her hurry.

She plugged the heater into the outlet, twisted the control to high and waited for the first waves of radiant heat to wash over her ankles. Instead she heard an ominous pop, and the nauseating smell of burning plastic rose. In the same split second the lights winked out. Only the remnants of gloomy daylight that managed to struggle in through the windows remained.

Clancey snatched the heater's plug from the outlet, apologized to the customers and ran for the basement electrical panel. But when she threw the switch that should have restored power to the circuit, it showed a dull red warning. She knew that wasn't a good sign, so she turned it off again and stood biting her lip. She could call an electrician, but it was Saturday. Heaven knew when she'd actually get action. And she certainly couldn't just leave things as they were.

So there was really only one option. She was going to have to go outside and tell Rowan that she'd just fried the electrical panel. And she would simply have to ask if he couldn't please do something about it, really soon.

CHAPTER EIGHT

AS SOON AS ROWAN SAW HER, he stopped trimming up the juniper shrub on the far corner of the lot and turned to watch, his eyes narrowed, as she ran toward him.

Clancey told herself that there was no real need to hurry. Why scare him out of his wits? She had the situation under control for the moment, at least. It wasn't as if flames were shooting up the staircase. *Yet*, she reminded herself.

So she kept running, and therefore was out of breath and fairly close to him before she realized the expression in Rowan's eyes was not apprehension at all, but appreciation. He seemed to be enjoying the sight of her, in narrow-cut tweed trousers and a soft green sweater. Especially the sweater.

That slowed her to a walk. She also folded her arms firmly across her chest, trying as best she could to make the action seem casual. It didn't work, of course. That merciless green gleam of laughter was in his eyes, and the first thing he said as she came up to him was, "I guess this means you're not running out here to fling yourself in my arms."

Clancey ignored that. She was almost panting—not so much from the exertion as from nerves—as she told him about the heater, the ominous pop, the smell of burning plastic and the red warning light when she'd tried to correct things.

Rowan rubbed the end of his nose with his index finger. For what seemed a very long time, he had no comment at all.

Clancey's self-control snapped. "If I was trying to burn the place down, I wouldn't be out here for help!"

"You've already made a fair start at it, that's sure." He stepped back and looked at the shape of the juniper again as if he didn't have another concern in the world. "So what are you planning to do now?"

Obviously he didn't intend to do anything about it, Clancey told herself. She turned on her heel, but had taken only two steps toward the house when she stopped in her tracks. What on earth could she do about the mess, after all? And what good was it going to do—aside from salving her pride, possibly—if she stamped back into the house like a baby elephant having a tantrum, if she couldn't think of anything constructive to do when she got there?

So she came back to his side. "Rowan," she said, "you can't seriously mean that you expect me to handle this—do you? This whole nonsense of inside and outside jobs was crazy from the beginning. It's your house, dammit! Would you just come in and look at the blasted thing?" She was shivering. Her sweater was thickly knit, but the cool breeze had no trouble slipping between the strands of yarn. Her hand was shaking as she reached for his sleeve. "Please? I'll—"

I'll do what? the little voice in the back of her brain asked frantically. *What sort of enticement can I offer him?*

"I'll sign the lease," she said. "Right now. Before you even come inside, if you like."

He gave a sort of snort. "How about adding an amendment to cover damages? By Christmas I won't have any house left."

She bristled. "This is not my fault, you know. If the place had adequate wiring, it wouldn't have happened."

"Clancey, no house has wiring that can stand up to three lamps, a cash register, a calculator, a heater and heaven knows what else, all plugged in to one outlet. How did you have it all wired, anyway? Six extension cords?"

She couldn't help looking a little guilty. He said something under his breath that she was glad she couldn't hear clearly and started for the house.

Clancey relaxed and tried not to smile as she followed him across the leaf-strewn lawn. It would be all right now.

The customers she'd left inside Small World seemed to have taken the sudden dusk as a challenge. One of them had chosen a collector's doll, the other had managed to find a book. Without thinking, Clancey flipped the button to turn on the cash register to ring up their purchases. There was, of course, no response from the machine, and she scrambled for a pen and a receipt book.

Rowan returned from the basement just in time to witness her confusion. "You might want to turn on a light," he suggested, tongue in cheek, "so you won't make mistakes in addition."

She glared at him. He dropped gracefully to the floor beside the misbehaving outlet and began to whistle softly. There wasn't a great deal of space behind the small counter to begin with, and one very solid male sitting cross-legged at her feet certainly didn't help the situation. The tuneless whistle was the final straw.

"You're the human calculator," Clancey snapped. "What's the sales tax on a hundred and thirty-nine dollars?"

Rowan stopped whistling long enough to tell her. Before she had the figure written down he'd interrupted himself again, just long enough to give her the total bill. "Can you handle making change," he asked politely, "or shall I tell you what that is, as well?"

She would have liked to kick him in the kneecap and then protest innocently that her foot had slipped in the confined quarters. But she restrained herself. "I can handle it just fine, thanks—if I can get the damned cash drawer open."

She'd never had to use the manual override before, and she congratulated herself for even remembering it existed. She was certain Rowan would have taken great pleasure in reminding her.

Thank heaven for a slow day, she was thinking as the two women departed, change and packages in hand. She settled herself on the high stool to watch as Rowan unscrewed the outlet. It wasn't that there was nothing else she could be doing, but the way his body was wedged against the counter, there was no way to get past him short of climbing over the cash register.

"Here's the problem," he said finally. "The outlet shorted out and sizzled even before the circuit breaker popped. Good thing you weren't standing in water when it happened."

He handed her the outlet. Even Clancey's inexperienced eyes could see the scorch marks. "Great," she muttered, holding it warily. "What do you expect me to do with this?"

"Throw it away. That's all it's good for." He tugged the connecting wires out into the open and bent them at sharp angles so the bare ends were well away from each other.

"Isn't that dangerous, leaving wires hanging loose like that?" Clancey asked.

"Not when the power is shut off."

"You're planning to leave it off? But I can't work without electricity!"

"Obviously. The outlet will have to be replaced."

"Oh," she said with relief. "And you don't carry one around with you, is that it?"

"Not generally. Well, I'm going back to my pruning."

"You can't mean you expect me to take care of this? Rowan, dammit—" Then she remembered she'd made a promise and hadn't yet kept it. Was that what he was waiting for? She scrambled through the papers in the cabinet under the cash register, found the lease and scrawled her name along the proper line without allowing herself to think it over any further. In any case, additional time to think wouldn't change anything, because she didn't have any options left. "There—I've signed." She thrust the paper at him. "That means repairs are up to you, inside and out. It's right there in section seven."

He sighed and took the paper out of her hand. "I was sort of afraid you'd do that."

Clancey blinked. "What do you mean?"

"Oh, let's just say I was beginning to look at the advantages of letting you stay."

She opened her mouth, but shock had robbed her of her voice. Before she found it again, he'd gone on.

"If you do manage to burn the place down, it's insured," he mused. "And if you don't—well, perhaps I could learn something from Leonard Schultz. Just pocket the lease payments, stop paying for taxes and upkeep, and let somebody else get the house, and the frustration, in three years the same way I did."

Clancey laughed. "You're no slum lord." She couldn't have explained why, but something about the way he had said those things convinced her that there wasn't a fragment of truth in any of them. Hank was wrong, she realized, and was letting his dislike of Rowan interfere with his judgment. "You couldn't just let the house sit here and rot. You have too much of a conscience."

Rowan sighed. "You're probably right. It would keep me awake nights if I stuck some other poor devil with this place."

So he was getting tired of it, she thought. He certainly didn't sound like the same man who'd strolled through the rooms that first day, unfazed even by a leaking roof, and announced that it was a great house. But then, she had to admit that she herself had suffered some small shifts in attitude about the place. She felt a tinge of horror, now, at the idea that she'd blithely planned to buy the house from Leonard Schultz someday and do the renovation herself. A little paint stripper, some bolts of wallpaper—that was all she'd thought it would take to restore long-gone elegance. She hadn't given a thought to unromantic projects such as ceilings and electrical wiring and plumbing. No doubt the hot-water pipes would burst any day now, and with the mushroom factor in full force, who knew where that might end?

But Rowan was no novice when it came to old houses. He would have realized the amount of labor a renovation entailed. This dispirited attitude of his must be only temporary, the result of unpleasant surprises coming one after another. And it was no wonder he felt that way, really. If he'd been able to plunge into work right away, while the project was new and his enthusiasm was fresh, things like this wouldn't have bothered him at all. She'd have bet on it.

She told herself not to feel guilty about Rowan's frustrations; it hadn't been her fault. Besides, now that she'd agreed to let him start to work inside as well as out, that enthusiasm of his would return with a burst. She was certain of that. She might wake up tomorrow morning to the sound of sledgehammers knocking out walls.

She looked at the scorched outlet box in her hand. "It's almost a relief, really," she said. "Maybe it's just that Halloween is only a few days off, but I'm beginning to wonder if the place is haunted."

Rowan snapped his fingers. "That's what it must be—Leonard put a hex on it!" He pushed himself to his feet and groaned as he flexed the knee that had been cramped against the wall.

"Rowan," she began as he headed toward the front door.

He turned, brows raised.

She was leaning on the counter, arms folded on the glass top. "You will let me know before you start doing anything major, won't you? I mean, I'd hate to come downstairs some morning desperate for coffee and find out you'd torn out the whole kitchen."

He smiled, not the mischievous grin, but the warm and devastating smile that could lighten up a room all by itself. "Don't worry about it," he murmured. His fingertips flicked across her cheek and settled warmly under her chin.

Clancey could feel her heartbeat quicken, and she was relatively sure he was aware of it, too, even before his mouth brushed hers. It was a soft, mobile kiss, over almost before it began—at least, the actual contact was quickly broken, though Clancey suspected the after-effects might persist for some time to come.

"You're a dear, Clancey Kincade," he murmured. "Where *did* you get that name, anyway?"

"It was my mother's maiden name," she managed to answer, through the electric ripples that seemed to be chasing each other around her body. "She always wanted a child named Clancey, and I came along first, so I got the honors. When my brother was born two years later, they named him Will. Not fair, was it?"

He smiled slowly. His fingertips began to move gently against the soft skin of her throat. "You'd rather have been named Will? Actually, I'd say it was a good thing you turned out to be a girl."

Now what kind of an answer was she supposed to make to that? She managed to croak, "Oh?"

The mischievous twinkle sprang into his eyes. "It was especially fortunate for Will. A boy called Clancey would have had a fight a week, living up to his name."

He was out the door, still smiling, before she could do more than clench her fist and shake it at him.

As she set about straightening merchandise on the shelves, Clancey found herself thinking that while it would be a nuisance to live in the midst of chaos for the next few weeks, it might actually be fun, too. If she couldn't keep the house herself—and she'd finally reconciled herself to that fact—then at least she'd be able to see it beginning to take shape. She couldn't help but wonder exactly what Rowan's vision for it was, and this would be her only chance to find out.

And if the work on the house meant she'd be seeing a great deal more of Rowan—well, she could manage to live with that, too.

CLANCEY WAS AS INTERESTED in art and theater and civic projects as anyone, but she had to admit that she wasn't enjoying the fund-raising banquet. Too many long hours and restless nights, topped off by a heavy meal and forced inactivity, had left her fighting a battle to keep her eyes open by the time the main speaker took the microphone.

She should have broken her date with Hank and taken Rowan up on the invitation he'd made when he came back from the hardware store with the new outlet. Chinese food, followed by a stroll to the ice-cream shop and a fast-paced game of gin rummy, might not have been the most glamorous program possible for a Saturday night, but it would have been far more to her liking than a dry ceremony honoring people she'd never met for accomplishments she didn't know anything about.

At least with gin rummy she would have been able to choose a comfortable chair.

Clancey told herself firmly that she shouldn't complain. So what if it was a less-than-exciting evening? It was for a good cause.

But as the speaker droned on, she couldn't help thinking that a different sort of companion would have helped matters. Someone to share a laugh with at the speaker's occasional light remark. Someone who'd at least glance at her once in a while and smile, to acknowledge that her presence was important to him.

She let her eyelids drift shut, and allowed her imagination to roam.

Someone who would hold her hand unobtrusively under the edge of the table, or put a casual arm across the back of her chair. Someone with dark hair and deep blue eyes, who she was certain would look wonderful in the severe black of evening clothes.

Someone like Rowan.

Her eyes snapped open just as the speaker's voice soared to a conclusion, but it took a moment for her to realize that everyone around her was applauding.

Someone like Rowan....

Clancey bit her lip and joined politely in the ovation.

"Dynamite speaker," Hank said in her ear.

Clancey nodded. She'd known that was what Hank would say. When he liked a speaker, the speech was "dynamite," when he didn't, it was "a loser."

That's not fair, Clancey told herself. She'd been seeing Hank for a year; of course she'd learned to predict his actions, and even his words sometimes. She'd met Rowan only weeks ago. He might be just as predictable, once she got to know him.

No. She shook her head ruefully. If there was one quality Rowan McKenna absolutely did not possess, it was predictability. Of that much she was certain. She'd often been annoyed with him, if not actually infuriated, but she'd never suffered a twinge of boredom in his presence.

When Hank took her home, Clancey invited him in for coffee, but was almost relieved when he refused. She was, however, surprised by his reasons.

"This house gives me the creeps after dark," he said, looking around the dim front hall with a shiver. "And the store does, too, when only the security lights are on—all those beady eyes staring at me." He put his arms around her. "I'll call you next week, maybe I'll have some time."

His kiss was pleasant, but it started no flickering fires in her veins and sent no shock waves along her nerves.

You can't have it both ways, Clancey, she told herself as she waved goodbye to him. She closed the front door and leaned against it for a moment. If just once in her life she had kissed Hank with real enthusiasm, who knew what might have happened? But they didn't have that type of relationship. They were friends. And it was too late now.

Because it was Rowan, and only Rowan, that she wanted.

She put her fingertips to her temples, trying to still the sudden ache that pounded there—the ache of certainty. When she'd told herself earlier today that having Rowan hanging around all the time would be bearable, she had been lying to herself. Seeing him regularly wouldn't be a trial but a treat, and she'd known that even then, in the secret corners of her mind. That was probably why she'd signed the lease. It wasn't because she wanted to see the changes in the house—she'd wanted to see Rowan.

Idiot, she told herself. And just what did she plan to do about it now? Run away? Throw herself at him?

To do either was sheer foolishness, that was certain, but even the less-drastic, in-between alternatives didn't sound much better. Christmas was still two months off; avoiding him was impossible, short of simply locking the doors of her business and walking away—and that was out of the question, of course. But if she made any sort of attempt to attract him, he couldn't possibly take her seriously. There was the lease, and the fact that she had signed it only under duress. He wouldn't forget how much she wanted to stay in this house, and how much her business depended on it. And he would assume—any man of sense would—that she was acting on those motives, and not for personal ones.

And what then? He would either play along, for his own unknown reasons, or cut her short. Either outcome would be unbearable.

Not only her head was hurting now, but her ears and her feet, as well. Clancey yanked the heavy gold disks from her earlobes, then kicked off her shoes and stooped to pick them up. She was considering throwing them at the mantel, just in case it might help relieve her frustration, when a voice came out of the darkness at the top of the stairs.

"Was that long sigh one of gratitude or disappointment?"

She spun around, mouth open, clutching her shoes to her chest. "What?"

Rowan came down to the landing and leaned against the newel post. "Because Hank left, I mean. Are you glad or sad?"

She swallowed hard. "I can't see that it's any of your business."

"Oh, it's not," he admitted cheerfully. "Mere idle curiosity. I didn't mean to watch, you understand, but I didn't think you'd appreciate it if I spoke up earlier, while he was kissing you."

Clancey raised her chin. "Don't hold your breath waiting for me to compliment your tact, Rowan."

He smiled a little and came on down the stairs into the soft glow of Small World's security lighting. "And I didn't think I'd better leave it till later, either. If you ran into something solid on the stairs in the dark, you might not have stopped running till you got to Texas."

"That's about the truth. What are you doing here, anyway?"

Rowan shrugged. "Since I couldn't play gin rummy by myself, I decided to take a look at the rest of the wiring."

"In the dark?" Clancey hoped that her voice held the right shade of incredulity and cynicism. It was certainly better than sounding awed and delighted that he would stick around and wait for her to come home from her date!

"Of course not. I took a break a while ago and fell asleep watching television. Did you know that there's something about your couch that induces unconsciousness?"

"You seem to be the only man who's ever experienced the problem."

Rowan started to smile. "Am I? That's certainly interesting. Of course, if I'd had your company and your help in staying awake..."

Clancey felt hot, embarrassed color sweeping up almost from her toes, and tried frantically to change the subject. "I didn't see your car anywhere."

"It's around behind the house. I didn't think there was any sense in causing talk."

"Trying to hide it will cause more."

The prospect didn't seem to bother him. "Well, at least this way it didn't cause you any trouble with Hank."

And seeing Hank kissing me obviously didn't cause you any trouble, either, Clancey thought. She said, a little more sharply than she'd intended, "It's none of your business whom I kiss good-night, Rowan."

"Certainly not," he said mildly.

Well, she hadn't expected anything different, had she? She mocked herself a little for even entertaining the idea of Rowan becoming passionately angry because she'd kissed another man. Rowan, furious because someone else had held her in his arms. Rowan, jealous because she'd smiled at a man who wasn't him—

"Do you hand out a lot of good-night kisses?" Rowan asked.

He sounded as if he was taking a sociological survey, Clancey thought, with no personal interest at all in the answer. She was suddenly so tired that she wasn't sure she could hold up her head for another minute. "Go home, Rowan," she ordered, and turned toward the staircase without waiting to see if he obeyed. "Dammit," she muttered under her breath as she climbed the first stair.

"Because if you do," he said from directly behind her, "I'd like to put in my application for one."

Clancey spun about. Her stocking-clad feet slid wildly on the worn old wood, and Rowan's arm came around her to hold her steady. Standing one step above him put her eyes directly on a level with his, but despite that, in the dim light that spilled over from the parlor, his face was too shadowed for her to see if there was mischief there, or not.

"You've still got the house key I gave you so you could lock up tonight," she said, almost at random.

"So I do." Now that she had her balance again, his fingers spread firmly across the small of her back, urging her down from the stair.

"I'd like it back." It was either step down or be pulled completely off her feet. Clancey decided to preserve her dignity, and descended.

"We'll talk about it," he muttered.

But talking was obviously not what he had in mind. And within a couple of minutes, even if Clancey had remembered the key, she couldn't have formed a coherent request for it. His back was against the paneled wall at the foot of the stairs, and Clancey, off balance and out of her depth, was leaning against him, pressed so close that every move, even each breath he took, was a sensual assault.

And by the time he released her, with a final gentle kiss, and let himself out the door, all she could do was sag onto the bottom stair and stare into the darkness.

If he had pushed just a little farther, she would have allowed him to take her upstairs to bed.

No, she admitted to herself. That wasn't quite true; it wouldn't have taken a push at all. If she could have managed to form the words, she would have *invited* him upstairs.

What in heaven's name was happening to her?

ROWAN DIDN'T return the key. But the next time she asked for it he solemnly promised that, like any conscientious landlord, he would knock before entering. With that, Clancey supposed she would have to be satisfied. It wasn't as if she anticipated waking in the middle of the night to find a mad rapist in her bed. If Rowan had wanted to make love to her, he knew how to manage it without any such show of force. She'd practically handed him a guidebook.

The cold, harsh fact was that he obviously didn't want to make love to her, or he'd have turned their incredible good-night kiss into something else altogether.

But that knowledge certainly didn't stop the physical reaction she suffered every time she saw him—the absurd lift of the heart, the breathless crush in her chest, the whistling sensation in her ears that was like the time she'd almost fainted. And she saw him often. He came nearly every evening and spent hours scraping wallpaper in one of the bedrooms upstairs.

When he appeared in the kitchen on Halloween, just as the store was about to close, she had to forcibly subdue the urge to run across the room and fling herself against him. He looked so good, and so comfortable, and so inviting. . . .

"You're earlier than usual," she said, and turned back to the box she'd been rummaging through. It was full of miscellaneous old stock that had simply been dumped together in the move, and treasures were nestling next to junk.

"Not really. It's already dark." He glanced at the coffeepot, which was just finishing its cycle, and came across to her. "What are you doing?" His hands came to rest gently on her shoulders.

She managed to conceal the thrill of anticipation that ran through her. "Looking for little toys and prizes to give to the neighborhood kids tonight when they come around trick or treating."

"I don't suppose you believe in giving them candy?"

"Darned right I don't—they'll get plenty of that as it is." She tossed a couple of small windup cars into the basket at her elbow.

"Mind if I stick around for the fun?"

She craned her neck to look at him, half surprised that he would even be interested.

"Well, there isn't much excitement on ghosts-and-goblins night in a high-rise apartment building," he said. "I've kind of gotten out of the habit, but it might be fun, with you."

It was a careless comment, but the idea of him wanting to share this one small thing with her made her start to glow, deep inside. In fact, the effect couldn't have been much more powerful if it had been a round-the-world cruise he was talking about instead of a couple of hours spent admiring small children who had dressed up in costumes to beg for treats.

It took every bit of self-control she had, but Clancey somehow kept her voice steady. "Sure. You can stay. You're right, you know. It's a lot more fun when you have someone to share it with."

He smiled a little, and he was rubbing his chin against her hair when Eileen poked her head around the corner of the door. Her eyes widened, but all she said was, "I've locked up, Clancey. Is there anything else before I go home?"

Rowan greeted her genially, let his hands slip slowly from Clancey's shoulders, poured himself a cup of coffee and started up the back stairs toward the waiting wallpaper.

"Not a thing," Clancey managed to say.

"Then I'll see you in the morning." Eileen paused while she was putting on her jacket. "What was he doing, anyway? Making sure *you* don't wear a toupee? It's no wonder he's not making much progress upstairs, is it?''

Clancey shrugged. "Well, he can't do much with all my stuff in the way. I certainly wouldn't appreciate it if he took the wallpaper off the ceiling right above my new television, you know."

Eileen looked at her for a long time, and said mildly, ''Boy, have you got it bad.''

Clancey didn't even hear the door close. She was too deeply immersed in the wave of knowledge that had poured over her like a cold shower. *Yes,* she thought, *I do, indeed, have it bad.*

She was physically attracted to him, there was no denying that. It was such a powerful attraction it practically robbed her of good sense. But she was no longer able to hide behind the conviction that physical attraction was all she felt.

The highlight of each day was now the moment he first appeared. The bright spot of her whole week was in knowing he'd be beside her tonight as she handed out these toys. Such feelings had very little to do with physical attraction.

Even if she never saw him again, never was close enough to touch him, still his well-being would remain in the front of her mind. It would be the thing she wished and prayed for. And she'd never entirely lose the electrical thrill that coursed through her every time she thought of him, whether he was anywhere nearby or not.

For that thrill wasn't born of physical attraction, nor even of overwhelming desire. It had come with loving him.

CHAPTER NINE

SHE WAS IN LOVE with Rowan McKenna.

Once that underlying truth was no longer deniable, Clancey's mind began to revolve with helpless questions. Exactly when had she let herself slip over the brink? In what moment had annoyance turned to attraction, and attraction mushroomed into love? On which day had Rowan become so incredibly important to her that now the mere thought of losing him was enough to make her throat go dry and her heart twist in pain?

The mere thought of losing him, she mused. As if one could lose what one had never possessed!

And what difference would it make, even if she could figure out precisely when it had happened? It couldn't be changed now.

But she found herself going back over it anyway, remembering how she had felt the first time he'd held her, outside her bedroom door the night the ceiling fell and she'd collapsed into his arms. She'd been seeking only comfort, or so she'd thought. But had she truly wanted something more than that, even then?

Afterward, guilt had overwhelmed her, for then she'd believed he was married. She'd told herself she was worried he'd get the wrong impression and think she was flinging herself at him. But might it actually have been something else she was feeling guilty about?

The subconscious knowledge that, married or not, she was very much attracted to him?

Or had it happened even before that—on that night they'd gone for a walk together and negotiated a compromise on the house? Rowan didn't have to compromise, she reminded herself, but he had given her a break, put her needs ahead of his own wishes—even his own rights. Of course her heart had been touched, but had it been at that moment when she began to fall in love with him?

It had started before the grand opening. She was reasonably sure of that, once she started looking honestly into her heart. For when Kaye McKenna had first come into the store, Clancey's instantaneous reaction had been confusion, an awkward mixture of liking the woman and at the same moment wishing she didn't. Half of her had been pleased at Kaye's thoughtful refusal to cause trouble, the other half had been childishly hoping the woman would commit some terrible social blunder so there would be a logical excuse for disliking her. The quandary had puzzled Clancey even then, and only now was it clear. She'd been happy that, if Rowan had to be married, at least his wife was a lovely person. And at precisely the same time she'd been frustrated and jealous over that very fact....

"What a schizophrenic reaction," she muttered to herself. "You're a case for the men in the white jackets, Clancey Kincade!"

And then there was Kaye's baby, and the way that oblivious infant had seized Clancey's attention. For the first few days—until she had found out he wasn't Rowan's after all—that child had never been far from Clancey's thoughts. Had she been reminding herself that if it was stupid to become attracted to a married man, then it was criminal to play games with one who had not only a wife but a child?

Or had she been dreaming of how it could have been if that child was not only Rowan's, but hers as well?

THE LAST GOBLIN of Halloween, a makeshift ghost who looked a bit old for the part, selected one of the curlicue turtle straws from Clancey's basket just as the clock struck eight and trick-or-treat time officially ended. "Hey, that's terrific," he said, holding it up for inspection. "Can I have another one?" There was a suspiciously adolescent crack in his voice.

Clancey laughed. "One to a customer, I'm afraid. Come back next year—" She bit her tongue hard as the ghost slithered off down the sidewalk, and said over her shoulder to Rowan, "I'm sorry. That invitation just slipped out." She didn't look at him.

"I wouldn't worry." His tone was casual. "By next Halloween he'll have forgotten all about it."

And what about you, Rowan? she wanted to ask. *Will you have forgotten all about it—and me?*

He eyed the substantial white blob as it drifted down the street and added, "In fact, he'll probably be off to college by then."

Clancey forced herself to smile. "There are always a few who are pushing the age limits."

"Pushing? I'd say he's giving them a knockout punch. Doesn't it bother you, the idea of opening your door to complete strangers wearing costumes, some of whom are taller than you?"

"I never really thought about it, I guess. Is that why you're hovering around looking menacing?"

"Oh, no. The dangerous look is my disguise, since I didn't have any other costume."

Ask a stupid question, Clancey thought. So much for the idea of his protective instincts kicking in where she was concerned!

"I didn't think of it in time," Rowan went on, "or I'd have dressed up as a murder victim and posed out front in a lawn chair."

Clancey turned off the porch lights. "Why?"

He went on happily, "So I could wait, very quiet and still, until the kids decided I was only a mannequin, before I'd move or groan or something."

"And scare them to death? Shame, Rowan."

"Not the really tiny ones," he said hastily. "But it would be fun to watch the big ones react. I'll bet that last ghost wouldn't have stopped running till he hit the end of the block."

"You won't give out much candy that way."

He grinned. "In that case, you should definitely approve of the plan. How about some dinner, Clancey? I still owe you a meal, and my table manners are once again adequate for public display."

It is not a good idea, she thought, *to let myself get in even deeper.* It would be far more sensible to decline gracefully, tell him he didn't owe her anything at all, and go back to the stockroom to price the new shipment that had just come in that morning. Stuffed clowns couldn't be sold until they were on display, that was certain—

"I'd like that," she heard herself saying, and hoped he couldn't hear the eagerness that lay beneath the easy words.

He took her to a steak house on the edge of town. "It's not exactly Pompagno's," he admitted as he hung up her coat, "but then we're not exactly dressed to their standards, either. At least, I'm not."

He was two steps behind her as they reached their table, and when Clancey turned to look at him, a bit surprised he wasn't right there to hold her chair, she discovered he was studying her clothes. She wasn't quite sure, though, if he was appraising the style of her coffee-brown trousers and bitter-chocolate silk blouse, or the way they fit her figure.

"So do you think they'd let me in?" she asked when he finally remembered to seat her.

"Who?" He sounded absentminded.

"The sniffy management at Pompagno's."

"Oh, them. If they didn't, it would be their loss. What sounds good, Clancey?"

It was the way the trousers fit, she concluded with a twinge of satisfaction. He might not even have noticed the style.

They ordered steaks—both medium rare—and baked potatoes and salads, and settled back over a glass of perfect red wine to wait. The steak house was busy, but Clancey was feeling no impatience.

Here and there was a family with children in costumes. "Half these people have probably just come from a party," Clancey speculated.

"Or are on their way to one. See the lady over there in pink plastic hair rollers? That's the scariest costume I've seen all night."

"I hate to break this to you, Rowan, but—"

"All right, I admit it would be worse if she'd add a facial mask and a nightgown. But not much worse."

Clancey sipped her wine and told herself it wasn't a good time to open her mouth; she was likely to put her foot firmly into it. But she couldn't resist. "Does that mean you have a lot of experience with facial masks and nightgowns and hair rollers?"

Her attempt to sound casual had been wasted effort, she decided as Rowan grinned at her. Clancey's insides began to tingle. There really was an unholy attractiveness to the man's smile.

"This would be the perfect time to regale you with horror stories about my three ex-wives, wouldn't it?" he said. "There was the one who used cod-liver oil on her face at bedtime, there was the one who munched a half-dozen raw onions every day because they have so many vitamins and there was the one who died mysteriously after—"

"In that case, she's not an ex-wife, she's a late wife."

"She generally was that, too," Rowan agreed. "Anywhere from thirty minutes to three hours late."

"I don't believe a word of this."

"Pity. I was just getting a good start."

"No ex-wives, then?"

"Sorry. None. No late wives, either. Just a mother so absentminded she used to get involved in constructing a new poem and forget all about her oatmeal mask till it was like concrete. And a sister who swiped our favorite shirts to sleep in, and spent so much time in the bathroom that my brothers and I threatened to move her mattress in there. And now, through no fault of my own, I'm acquiring a collection of sisters-in-law, too."

Clancey smiled at the note of self-pity in his voice. "Somehow, I don't think you're entirely unhappy about that."

"There are a few advantages," he admitted. "The good things are a little difficult to see on holidays, though, when the crowd is so thick that you can't get through the house."

Clancey said, with just a trace of yearning in her voice, "Is everyone together for holidays, then?"

He nodded. "Usually we all go home to Wisconsin. Not this year, though—everybody's coming here next month. In theory it's to celebrate Thanksgiving Day, but that's only an excuse. Actually, it's to spoil the new baby." He refilled her wineglass from the bottle at his elbow. "How about your family? You sounded a bit— I don't know—envious, perhaps."

"Downright jealous," she admitted. "My parents gave up the fast lane a few years ago and moved to Florida to manage an apartment complex near where my brother lives."

He nodded. "So when the holidays come, they're busy getting snowbirds settled for the winter."

"Exactly. And I can't leave here at holidays, because it's my busiest season, too. So we celebrate by mail and telephone, and I always go visit for a week or two in February, when things quiet down after inventory. This year—" She stopped abruptly. If there was one thing she didn't want to talk about tonight it was moving Small World. She certainly didn't want Rowan to think she was hinting, or begging, or even feeling sorry for herself. So she grasped for another subject. "I thought the roofers were supposed to start soon."

Rowan grimaced. "Don't remind me. The sort of excuses these people make, it's a wonder they can stay in business. For all I know it will be next spring now by the time they get around to it, and in the meantime the whole house is going to keep getting soggier."

"I see," Clancey said thoughtfully. "You aren't going to put up the new ceiling until you know it's going to stay dry. Well, that makes sense, I suppose."

"I know it's a mess, Clancey—"

"Oh, I wasn't complaining. I just think it's a shame, because when spring comes and the roof gets done, I suppose you'll be busy with everyone's income tax and won't have time to do anything."

He released a long sigh. "It is my busy time of year."

Clancey leaned back in her chair for the waiter to place her salad plate, and admitted, "I can't help but think about what could be done with that house. Every time I walk through it something else occurs to me." That was the understatement of the year, she reflected. She still remodeled that house every night as she drifted off to sleep.

"Like what?"

She paused with a forkful of spinach halfway to her mouth. "You're serious?"

"Of course. Not only are two heads better than one, but if there are things glaringly wrong with the place, you probably know what they are, since you've had to live with them."

She looked doubtful. "I don't know about that—I certainly didn't anticipate the problem with the wiring." She looked thoughtfully down at her salad, and then at him. "It's to be just a house, right? Or are you planning to put your offices downstairs?"

It might have been her imagination, but she thought he shuddered a little at the idea. "No," he said. It was firm.

"It's difficult to call in sick when you live above the shop," Clancey agreed. "Particularly if you aren't really sick. Well, with that in mind, I'd make the upstairs kitchen into a laundry room. Then I'd gut the downstairs kitchen and start from the bare walls, so I'd end up with a work space any gourmet would love to use."

He looked doubtful.

For a moment Clancey had been caught up in her own fantasy, picturing herself in that brand-new kitchen, stirring and chopping and singing in pure pleasure. "Well, you did ask me what I would do," she pointed out stiffly. "I suppose you eat out of brown paper bags all the time?"

"Mostly. But go on."

She hesitated. Her eyes were stinging a little, as if the onions she'd been dicing in that daydream had been real ones. This was only going to cause pain. It would have been better to pretend that she hadn't given it a thought. She shook her head a fraction.

"What about the two little rooms at the back of the second floor?" he prompted.

"The servants' rooms? Sorry. Never thought about them."

The waiter brought their steaks. Rowan cut the first slice, chewed it thoughtfully and said, "Storage, I suppose. They're too small for anything else."

Clancey almost dropped her fork. "Storage? How much stuff have you got, anyway—more than will fit in the attic? Don't you have the slightest spark of imagination, Rowan McKenna?"

His eyes widened. "Now what does that mean?"

"Knock the wall out between them and turn the space into a giant master bathroom."

He blinked. "Clear at the back of the house?"

"Why not? It's next to the nicest bedroom."

"Not the biggest."

"But it has a fireplace. You wouldn't exactly want that in the nursery, would you?" She felt herself start to color a little, and plunged on before that merciless teasing light could come alive in his eyes. "Besides, you could put walk-in closets in the new space and have a dressing room—make it a real master suite. That way, the bedroom doesn't have to be so huge."

"With a whirlpool tub, I suppose?"

"Of course. And an exotic shower, and lots of cabinets."

He nodded thoughtfully. "And put the nursery where the bedroom is now."

This time there was no doubt about the flush rising in her cheeks, but she couldn't simply ignore the question, so she said coolly, "I suppose that would be the best choice. The other big rooms upstairs all have balconies. The master bedroom could be furnished with—" Then she broke off, remembering that it might not be quite safe to share her image of the perfect bedroom with him, because her vision of that room was imagined not for a single man, but for a couple.

A couple who would nestle together beside the snapping fire on cold winter evenings, and sit in the overstuffed chintz chairs by the bay window to have coffee in the mornings, and share the king-size tester bed....

A very specific couple. A strawberry blond woman and a man with very dark hair and eyes that were a strange shade of blue-green, eyes that could light with mischief in the fraction of an instant.

That in itself made her realize how slowly and completely Rowan had crept into her heart. The fact that she'd imagined him there beside her for all time—and didn't even realize she was doing it because it felt so natural—was almost terrifying.

"What were you saying?" Rowan asked politely.

"Nothing much." Clancey dug her fork into her baked potato as if it was an enemy. "Whatever it was seems to have escaped me at the moment. Now about that little room downstairs, right by the front door..."

IT WAS ALMOST THE MIDDLE of November, and autumn had come with a vengeance. On some days the wind howled around the house, tugging at the few brown leaves that still clung stubbornly to the trees, an unpleasant reminder of the arctic air that was on its way. And yet other days were soft and mild, and Clancey thought longingly of picnics, and swinging in the park, and digging in the flower beds by the front porch.

It was an almost physical pain to realize she'd never know what sort of flowers might come up there in the spring, what bulbs had been planted there long ago by some unrecorded hand. She would never add her own favorites—red tulips and yellow daffodils and blue balloon flowers.

Somewhere else, she told herself, there'd be a place where she could do that. A little house, not nearly so big as this, she could take care of by herself, with a flower bed and a patch of lawn.

But it was no comfort to think of things like that. For it wasn't houses or flower beds or lawns that made her ache with longing. It was Rowan. And after she and Small World moved, she'd never see him again. He would have no reason to contact her, and she'd have no excuse to seek him out....

Taxes, she thought. She'd always managed to do the bookkeeping and paperwork herself, but it honestly was getting beyond her. She could hire him to take care of it for her.

"Don't be foolish," she muttered. "What good do you think that would do?" There wouldn't be much comfort in sitting across a desk from him and watching while he calculated how much money she owed the federal government. Merely seeing his face would be a poor substitute for all she wanted. In the long run it would only increase her pain.

And so she shivered on the cold days when winter's approach was threateningly near, and rejoiced on the warm ones, when she could pretend that moving day was a long way off. And whenever she saw Rowan, each time he touched her, whether it was a casual finger brushing against her hair or cheek, or the occasional kiss—more casual and careless than passionate, to her regret—she could feel herself sinking a little deeper into the quicksand.

Still, she treasured each encounter, and stored away every smile and touch against a time when there would be no more.

IN THE MIDDLE OF ONE of those bright and beautiful afternoons Kaye stopped by to look at toys, and to invite Clancey to join in the celebration she was planning for Thanksgiving Day. "It occurred to me you might be alone," she said. "And we'd really love to have you complete our circle."

The request sent Clancey's heart tripping double-time. Was this really Rowan's idea, disguised as Kaye's, asking her to join what was very plainly a family holiday? And even if it had been Kaye's own idea, surely she would have checked it out with him before inviting Clancey, and so he must have approved. Did this mean that Kaye—and others, too—actually thought of them as a couple, somehow?

Good manners forced her to say, "Oh, Kaye, that's lovely. But you'll have a houseful of family."

"Family and friends. There's plenty of room for one more. Honestly, Clancey, what on earth would you do instead?"

"Get some extra sleep. Catch up on my laundry...."

Kaye began shaking her head. "No. I won't hear of it. Holidays shouldn't be wasted on ordinary chores, and you can't spend Thanksgiving Day alone, Clancey. You must come and join us. Besides, the rest of the family can't wait to meet the only person who's ever been able to keep Rowan from getting what he wanted." She picked up a bright picture book and flipped the pages.

"Not for long," Clancey said, almost under her breath.

"Oh, that doesn't matter. It's still quite an accomplishment. Are you looking for a new place for your store yet?"

"I haven't had much time. So far it doesn't seem promising."

"It would be interesting to see what would happen if you just staged a sit-down strike and refused to move," Kaye speculated.

"I couldn't do that to Rowan." Clancey's voice was deeper than usual, steeped with sincerity, and only when she finished straightening the racks of cassette tapes did she see the unmistakable curiosity in Kaye's eyes. "I mean," she added hastily, "he's already put himself to far more aggravation than most people would, for a stranger. I wouldn't dare cause him more trouble."

"I see," Kaye said mildly.

Clancey had the uncomfortable feeling she wasn't deceiving anyone.

Kaye put the book back on the shelf and turned to the teddy-bear tree. "How are the petitions being received?"

"Very well, I think. No one has taken offense, and most of my customers seem to like the idea of enlarging the historic district. Do you really think you can pull it off?"

Kaye smiled. "Of course. I did it a few years ago, to get our house in. But this time it's a little more urgent, I'm afraid. You know the city council is thinking of building the new civic center on this side of town?"

"Here? Why?"

"You might well ask. I can see it now—a concrete block monstrosity in the middle of a Victorian neighborhood. There are dozens of more suitable places."

Clancey's brow furrowed. "But rather than oppose the civic center—"

"Politically unwise," Kaye agreed.

"You're going around the back way, aren't you?"

Kaye nodded. "If the preservation guidelines are extended, they can't put in a modern building."

"It would be stupid, anyway, to tear down wonderful old houses. There are blocks in this city that could be firebombed without any loss."

"Well, it wouldn't be the first stupid thing the city ever did. But it takes time, Clancey. Time and interested people. If you still want an old house, I know of several around here that could be purchased reasonably right now."

And then I'd never have to move again, Clancey thought.

She could renovate and remodel to her heart's content; she could stock up all the inventory she wanted and know she'd never have to pack it in a truck and move it somewhere else. By staying in the same area it would be easier to retain her customers. She wouldn't lose all the effort and expense of the advertising she'd done in the past few weeks.

And she could also watch what Rowan did to his house, she reflected. She would see the new roof go on next spring; she would see the new materials as they were carried inside. She could imagine, from that, what he was doing and what the house must look like as each stage of construction progressed.

Be honest, Clancey, she told herself. That would be the biggest advantage, as far as you're concerned— being close to Rowan.

And perhaps it would be the biggest disadvantage, as well. To watch longingly as he remade the place into a home would be very difficult, knowing as she did that it could never be her home. And when the inevitable day came that he brought some other woman to the house—and perhaps made the nursery he had talked of into reality—that would be unbearable.

"I think I'll be looking for a space in a strip mall, actually," Clancey said. She managed to keep her voice level. "It's much more practical."

Kaye nodded. "Of course it would be." She sounded just a little disappointed. "Well, you must do as you want."

But what Clancey wanted had very little to do with it, she thought, wrapping up the toy Kaye had chosen. If her desires had any bearing at all, things would be arranged differently.

For what Clancey wanted was not just any old house, or even this specific old house. It was Rowan she wanted. It was Rowan who was important. And she wanted him more than she'd ever wanted anything else in her life.

CHAPTER TEN

CLANCEY WENT FOR A WALK that evening, enjoying the sharp night air, the clarity of the stars above her, the feeling of absolute aloneness. At least when she was by herself she didn't have to try to keep smiling to put a good face on things. As pleasant as Kaye was, she was sometimes uncomfortably acute. The problem of what Clancey was going to do about Thanksgiving Day was a good example. Kaye's invitation was special, something to be treasured whether it had anything to do with Rowan or not. Clancey hated her lonely holidays, far from her family, and there was nothing she would like better than to be part of a warm and loving circle.

But even loneliness might be less painful than spending a holiday in the same group with Rowan. It would be hard to be with his family, and yet not really be part of it. It would be very difficult to get to know his relatives for a few precious hours, and then go home alone.

Wouldn't it be better to spend the holiday as she usually did than to allow herself to fantasize, knowing that the fairy tale would end?

But Kaye wouldn't take no for an answer. If necessary, she hinted, she would send a kidnapping force.

It will be all right, Clancey told herself as she walked home through the moonlight. *Maybe you'll hate his mother. Maybe you'll hate them all.*

Right, she added ironically. Just as much as she disliked Kaye! Just as much as she detested Rowan....

She'd left the porch lights on, and as she came down the street the house seemed to glow a little warmer in greeting. Under the new coat of paint the whole structure seemed to stand taller, as if it was able to be proud of itself again.

Once the new roof was on, the house would be just as solid as the day it was built. And if Rowan devoted some time and energy to replacing the gingerbread trim that must have accented the porch and the gables when the house was new...

Would he take the restoration to such lengths, she wondered. Or did he prefer a simplified, more modern approach? She couldn't blame him if he did. It would certainly require less upkeep. Painting gingerbread every year or two was not exactly to everyone's taste. And what about the interior? Would he restore the missing grandeur there, or streamline the whole thing into a sleek contemporary adaptation of Victorian beauty?

She reflected suddenly that he really hadn't said, in their chat over dinner on Halloween night, what he intended to do. Clancey had done most of the talking, afraid that if she lost control of the conversation it would lead in directions she didn't want to go.

Now she wished she had come straight out and asked him what his plans were. She did have an interest in the house; surely he wouldn't have objected to telling her what he planned to do with it.

Then, on further consideration, she shook her head. "It might be better not to know," she muttered. "Just in case he plans to do something crazy—like turn the parlor into a wet bar with a hot tub big enough to seat eight.''

That was the gaudiest, most tasteless decorating scheme she could think of at the moment, and the very idea amused her. No, he wouldn't do anything like that, she thought. Rowan wasn't the wet-bar-and-crowded-hot-tub type. Now if it was a glass of champagne and a single intimate friend in a whirlpool—

Stop it, she warned herself. *Just because you'd like to be that intimate friend doesn't mean Rowan feels the same way.*

But once she had allowed the seductive image into her mind, it wasn't easy to push it away.

IT SNOWED A LITTLE on the Friday afternoon before Thanksgiving Day. Clancey thought it was great. The sky might be gray and gloomy, the wind cutting and the general atmosphere dreary, but it always took a snow before people truly got into the mood to shop for Christmas. And if the snow came a full week before the traditional start of the shopping season, so much the better for sales and profits in the long run.

Eileen, on the other hand, made little effort to hide her disgust. ''It's too early for this,'' she wailed. ''It's fine for you to be chortling about the crummy weather—you have to stay here all evening, anyway. But it's my night off!''

The reminder sobered Clancey a little. Small World had always been open late on Friday nights. It was one of the better retail times in this particular business, because paychecks were fresh and couples were free to shop together. But that didn't make the twelve-hour day any easier to get through, and looking at the calendar and seeing how many of those days still lay ahead made her feel grim. If only she had felt free to hire another full-time assistant.

"Snow," Eileen muttered irritably. "On my night off."

"Don't complain too much," Clancey recommended as she retreated behind the cash register. "You might tempt me to revise the December schedule so you can work a few extra days." It was chilly by the front door, and she folded her hands around her coffee mug to capture the warmth from the china. Rowan had replaced the problem outlet, but she hadn't dared plug the portable heater in again for fear of another blackout. "Or, let's see. I suppose I could get violently ill all of a sudden and make you stay tonight while I go drink chicken soup and watch a bad movie."

Eileen's eyes widened. "You wouldn't dare. I have a—"

"Oh? A heavy date, were you going to say? I thought you were finished with all of that. Don't tell me you're still seeing the kamikaze driver from the supermarket."

Eileen's cheeks had turned ever-so-slightly pink. "Who? Oh, no. I sort of took your advice this time."

Clancey tried to remember which advice Eileen might have taken to heart, and gave it up as an impossible job. "I hate to remind you," she said finally, "but it's past your quitting time."

Eileen's dust cloth didn't even pause. "He's picking me up here."

The fact threw light on one thing that had been puzzling Clancey for half an hour. She hadn't asked Eileen to dust the bookshelves. It was a job Eileen hated. But from there she had a good view of the front sidewalk.

"I actually get to meet one of your dates? In that case, it must be true love!"

"Who's in love?" Rowan asked from the doorway between dining room and kitchen. "Eileen?"

Neither of them had heard him come in, but there he was, leaning against the jamb, his soft cap pulled down over his forehead, the shadow of the brim making his eyes look even darker.

I'm grateful, Clancey told herself. *I'm very glad he doesn't seem to think it was possible I was talking about me.*

But it annoyed her, nevertheless—the fact that she was apparently of so little interest to him he didn't even consider she might have someone important in her life.

Eileen had turned a charming shade of rose pink. "Of course I'm not in love," she protested. "It's just a date, that's all. And here he comes, so if you embarrass me, either one of you—"

The rest of the threat hovered in the air as the front door began to open.

Clancey sat back on the stool behind the cash register with her elbows on the counter and propped her chin in her hands, watching the door with undisguised curiosity.

It was perhaps fortunate she'd had such little time to conceive notions of what Eileen's new boyfriend would look like, for the man who came into sight would have met none of them. He was older than Clancey would have expected. He was also shorter and stockier. And the top of his head was bare and pink and surrounded by a rim of dark brown hair. It almost looked as if it had been polished.

Clancey couldn't help herself. Her jaw dropped.

The man smoothed his coat lapel—his suit had been carefully and expensively tailored to make him look taller and slimmer, Clancey decided—and said tentatively, "Is Eileen here?"

All she could do was point into the parlor.

Rowan obviously had better control of himself; he came forward with hand outstretched. "Good to see you, Lawrence," he said cheerfully.

Lawrence shook hands, and then, as if it was an irresistible urge, he ran a hand over the top of his head, nervously stroking the smooth pinkness. It looked to Clancey as if he wasn't used to the feel of naked skin, or perhaps as if he wasn't quite sure what Rowan was likely to say about it.

That was when Clancey remembered the advice Eileen must have been referring to. At least he could take off the toupee, Clancey had told her once; other men couldn't shed their shortcomings so easily.

Good heavens, she thought. *I wonder how she managed to make him give it up.*

Eileen excused herself to hang up her dust cloth and wash her hands, and Clancey listened in dumbfounded silence as the two men compared notes on the mayor's latest, and riskiest, political stand. Rowan had said something about hanging around city hall, Clancey remembered. But was there no one he didn't know?

After the couple had gone, Rowan leaned against the counter beside her and said thoughtfully, "I wonder if Eileen likes the idea of being first lady of the city someday."

"I doubt she's given it any— You mean Lawrence might run for mayor?"

Rowan nodded. "Next election. He's one of the powers behind the scenes right now, just biding his time. I've already agreed to be finance director for his campaign. I wonder if Eileen is the one who persuaded him to acquire the natural look."

"I wouldn't be surprised if she was." Clancey's voice was dry.

"Probably so. Well, if that's the case, she may have quite a future as a political adviser, too. That toupee was his biggest handicap."

"Just as long as she waits till after Christmas to take on the job," Clancey muttered.

Rowan grinned. "He may have looked just a little dizzy about her, but Lawrence has his head on straight—he wouldn't give up common sense for any woman. Need anything from the hardware store?"

Clancey shook her head.

"I'll be back soon, then. Want to go out for something to eat later?"

"It's my night to stay open till nine, so I've got a sandwich." She wished that she could agree—just close the place down and go off with him right now, if he liked. But she couldn't, and the disappointment made her say perversely, "Besides, I thought you came to work on the wallpaper."

"I did. But I remembered when I got here that I broke my scraper last night. I wouldn't get far with only my fingernails, I'm afraid." He dropped a kiss on her cheek and then he was gone, leaving her heart rocking like a boat in a storm.

It wasn't fair, she thought, that such a fleeting contact could have so deep an impact on her. Clancey supposed she ought to be grateful there hadn't been a repetition of that steamy good-night kiss. The results could have been nothing but embarrassing for her, because she certainly couldn't have kept her poise through another one of those. It was difficult enough to stay calm and casual through the ordinary things—the touch of his hands as he helped with her coat, the flick of his fingertips against her cheek, the sudden devastation of his smile....

The waiting, when she knew that she would see him soon, when every footstep made her look up with hope...

But tonight, the masculine feet that stamped across the front porch and sent her heart rate skipping turned out to be Hank Gleason instead.

He brushed snowflakes off the shoulders of his camel-colored topcoat and smiled at her. "It's turning into quite a storm out there, Clancey. I suppose you ordered this to get people in the holiday spirit?"

"It doesn't seem to be working," she said lightly. "I've only had a few customers tonight. The others must all be at home by their fires."

"That's where I'm headed, too. Finally—after almost a month—my client's tax troubles are taken care of."

"That's good. Did you get him cleared?"

Hank nodded. "Compromise and negotiation, that's the answer. Since I hadn't had a minute for you in so long, I thought I'd better stop by and catch up. I've missed you, Clancey."

She smiled, rather sadly.

Hank propped his elbows on the counter and leaned confidentially toward her. "This month has made me think about a lot of things. I've realized, for one, that I haven't been paying enough attention to you."

What had brought this on? Clancey wondered. She said uneasily, "Sometimes it just doesn't work out. We're both busy people, Hank."

He nodded and looked around the shop, at the multitude of Christmas toys and decorations. "You can say that again. Must have taken days to get all this stuff put up." He gestured at the row of stockings hung suggestively from the mantel, and picked up a teddy bear in a Santa T-shirt from a nearby pile. "I'm surprised you went to all the bother."

Clancey shrugged. "I can't sell merchandise straight out of the shipping boxes, you know. Not unless I want a reputation as a discount store. I'll just have to pack it all up again sooner or later, if it doesn't sell."

"Sooner or later?" he repeated. "Does that mean McKenna has decided to let you stay a while?"

"No. I still have to be out on January first."

"You signed that short-term lease, then?" Hank shook his head and said, almost to himself, "It still doesn't make sense."

"Signing it?"

"No. Kicking you out. If he'd left the three-year lease in place, of course, you could have gotten nasty about it. But now that you've agreed to the shorter time, I'd think it would be smarter to let you stay a while and rent by the month with no guarantees of possession. It's a delicate spot he's in at the moment. Without a tenant, he's not going to get the maximum out of the place when he sells it."

"Sells it?" Clancey shook her head in confusion. "Rowan's not going to sell it. He's going to renovate it and move in."

"I suppose he told you that?"

"Yes."

"Directly? He said exactly that?"

''How should I remember exactly how he said it? What are you talking about, Hank? Where did you get the idea he was planning to sell?''

''It took me a while to figure out, you see. He's got better political connections than I do, for one thing.''

Political connections, she thought blankly. Did Hank mean things like Lawrence, and the campaign that would come up someday for the mayor's seat? What was wrong with that?

''And little deals like this stay hidden pretty well down at city hall,'' Hank went on.

Something seemed to echo in the back of her mind. *You hear lots of things when you hang around city hall,* Rowan had said once. She shook her head. What did that have to do with anything?

''You've heard about the civic center?'' Hank said.

''Of course. Are they still talking about building it on this side of town?'' Kaye would like to know if that was so, she thought.

Hank shook his head. ''Not on this side of town, exactly.'' He pointed at the floor. ''They're going to build it right here.''

Clancey's throat closed up till all she could manage was a whisper. ''You mean this house?''

''This block,'' Hank said impatiently. ''No wonder McKenna bought himself an old, decrepit house in the middle of a decaying neighborhood. I've always thought that was strange. He's too smart with his money to do that kind of thing for kicks. But now I know why.''

She shook her head. ''You've got to be wrong, Hank.''

''Honey, I've seen the list of sites.''

Clancey swallowed hard. "No," she said. It was almost a plea. "He wouldn't do all this work and then let the city condemn it."

Hank looked around. "All of what work?" he asked bluntly. "I don't see a lot of evidence."

They'd been through this same argument once before, Clancey reminded herself. "Hank, last time we had this talk, you thought Rowan wanted to get rid of me just so he could rent to less-particular tenants."

He shrugged. "That was before I got the facts about the civic center. And before I found out that McKenna's been looking into a whole lot of other properties around here, too."

Clancey blinked. "He has?"

"Yes, he has. And what would he do with them all, Clancey? A man can only live in one house at a time."

And this one, she remembered, he'd bought before he'd even been inside. She'd thought it a quixotic impulse, odd and eccentric. But when she considered it, what kind of fool was crazy enough to invest perfectly good money in a house without even knowing if it was livable?

He'd said it was a great house and that it was everything he had hoped for, and more. But what, precisely, had he meant? The house of his dreams? An architectural wonder? Ideally suited for his purposes?

And just what purposes had he been thinking of?

"What's he done to the place? Anything that amounts to much?"

"Paint," Clancey began automatically.

Hank nodded. "That was smart. It increases the curbside appeal, for when the appraiser comes around and estimates how much they'll have to pay to get the place. The better it looks, the higher the first offer will be and the better the deal he can negotiate. Anything else?''

She shook her head slowly. "Not really. The roof..."

Hank chewed on his bottom lip. "That surprises me. I can't see that kind of work returning a profit.''

The shock was lessening now, as the realization sank slowly into Clancey's brain that Hank's arguments actually made sense.

The roof, she thought. Rowan had complained about the workmen and the delays. In truth, though, there was no evidence whatsoever that he'd even talked to a contractor.

But why would he say he had, if he hadn't? What would he have to gain from the lie?

Delay, she found herself thinking. All sorts of work needed to be done, from the missing bedroom ceiling on down, but until the leaky roof was replaced even Clancey had agreed that it made no sense to do much of it. And so he could slide by with doing nothing at all and avoid all the questions about why, if he was so eager to renovate the place, he was making so little progress.

Come on, Clancey, she told herself. *Hank's wrong, that's all. Rowan's been scraping wallpaper for days on end.*

That nagged at her a little, too. She wasn't quite sure why.

The fact that he'd been so silent about his plans for the house took on ominous implications once she started to think about it. Was it possible there were no plans, after all? Was it possible that he had just been letting her babble, not because he was interested in another point of view but just to fill up time and prevent her from asking about his own designs?

He was going to live here, she'd told Hank just minutes ago. But had Rowan ever actually said that?

Why do people usually buy houses? he'd said when she first asked about his plans. He'd answered a question with another question, not with a statement that tied him down. Had he ever actually committed himself? She couldn't remember; she'd assumed that her answer was the correct one, and she hadn't given it another thought.

When she'd asked him not to tear out the kitchen without warning her, he'd smiled and told her not to worry. What, exactly, had he meant?

He'd talked of budgets and time schedules, but those things could have dual meanings. Had he ever said anything about actually renovating the house?

Oh, in vague terms, he had. He'd talked of the modern equivalent of ceiling plaster, for instance, and how difficult it would be to install against the irregular old timbers. But had he ever said, *This is what I'm going to do?*

Not that Clancey could remember.

Was it possible she had been so very wrong?

She remembered Kaye's comment that Clancey was the only person who'd ever kept Rowan from getting what he wanted. She'd thought Kaye meant that he was impatient to get the necessary work done and move in. But had she meant instead that Clancey was standing in the way of his profits? And hadn't Kaye said something that day, as they drank tea while Rowan finished taking out the fallen ceiling, about his destructive instincts? Had there been some hidden meaning in her banter then?

Did Kaye know what he was planning? Had she decided on her quiet, indirect approach to opposing the civic center because if she took a more public stand she'd also be loudly opposing her brother-in-law?

Rowan had the connections to know what was going on at city hall; he'd said so himself. Besides, newcomers to the field of politics weren't generally asked to help run campaigns. If a site had been chosen for the civic center, it wouldn't be unlikely that Rowan would know which one, on that list of possibilities, it would be. Projects like that were planned years in advance, sometimes. He'd have had plenty of time to act.

And what if he had decided to capitalize on the knowledge? An investment of a few thousand dollars, tied up for a matter of months, and then a tidy profit, collected from city funds. It was unethical, at best. In most cases it was illegal to profit like that from inside knowledge of government business, to take advantage of public trust to defraud the taxpayer.

Not Rowan, her heart was whispering. *He wouldn't do that—would he?*

Her head was swimming, and a cold drop of sweat was trickling down her spine with agonizing slowness.

"He did offer to let me stay on." She was almost unaware of saying it aloud. *There would be advantages to letting you stay,* he'd said—something like that. She'd thought at the time it was only a bit of black humor, a reaction to the booby traps that seemed to be waiting all over the house.

"I wouldn't advise you to take the offer," Hank said. "Without a lease he can evict you anytime. And when they finally move on this project, they won't want delays."

Clancey shook her head. "No. I wouldn't stay."

Hank looked worried. "I didn't mean to upset you," he said awkwardly. "I thought it would be some comfort to know exactly what was going on."

She forced herself to smile. "Yes. Of course it is."

Hank wasn't even off the porch before Clancey climbed the stairs, hand trembling against the banister, to see what Rowan had accomplished in the past ten days in the little bedroom where he'd been stripping wallpaper. It was his business and no concern of hers, she'd told herself, and once all her possessions had been stacked in a corner and covered with plastic to protect them, she hadn't even looked in again. But now she found herself wondering what he'd been doing up there for a couple of hours every day. In that amount of time the wallpaper should be gone and the mess cleaned up. It should be ready for paint or new paper....

It wasn't. In fact, the walls looked as if they'd developed a bad case of chicken pox, with eruptions from the size of a saucer all the way up to three feet in diameter. In fifty different places the uneven surface of the dull yellow paint had been broken and the layers of wallpaper underneath partially scraped away. The walls were stained with dirty water and the remnants of old paste and glue.

And in the center of the room were a couple of boxes. They were Clancey's, part of her collection of odd and unusual toys. She'd checked that they were sealed, and had stacked them herself so they'd be out of Rowan's way.

Now they were open, and the packing tissue pulled back.

Fury rose in her, bringing a harsh metallic taste to her mouth. So this was what Rowan had really been doing. He'd been killing time, playing with toys, and creating only the illusion of renovation, so that when an appraiser walked through he could point out the house's potential, and the work already done, and the value that would be destroyed if it was to be taken away from him.

Clancey turned aside, feeling sick. Eileen had noticed, weeks ago, how slowly things were progressing, and put her finger squarely on the reason—Rowan wasn't working very hard. If it had been so obvious to her, why hadn't Clancey seen what was happening?

"Because I didn't want to see it," she muttered. "That's what you get for falling in love before you check out the facts, Clancey Kincade! You did it with the house, you've done it with Rowan—"

No wonder he'd agreed to let her stay those few weeks till Christmas, for now she remembered the other half of that deal—her promise not to sue. By letting her stay, he'd prevented the lawsuit she'd threatened to file—a legal action that would have caused nagging delays and fatal publicity.

She managed to fight off tears, but only by reminding herself that Rowan would come back sooner or later. She didn't want to explain herself or suffer his sympathy.

When he came in, she was standing behind the cash register, hands folded, looking into space, wishing she could run somewhere very far away and hide her head until she felt less like a fool.

He set a big bag down on the counter beside her and said with an easy grin, "I got two scrapers this time."

Clancey bent over suddenly to straighten out the stack of bags on the bottom shelf. It was the best excuse she could find to make sure he had no opportunity to repeat that casual kiss-on-the-cheek routine of his, and to hide the bleakness in her eyes. "In case another one breaks?" she asked in almost a monotone.

His eyes darkened a little as she dodged away. "No, in case you decide to help." But there wasn't quite so much humor in his voice. "I also got some Christmas lights on sale. You don't mind if I put them up on the porch rail, do you?"

"You mean tonight?"

"Or tomorrow, when I can see what I'm doing," he countered. "What difference does it make when I put them up?"

Clancey shrugged. "None. Why don't you stop playing house, Rowan? I'm not interested anymore."

He stopped digging boxes of lights out of the bag. "What the hell does that mean?"

She raised her chin. "Putting up Christmas lights doesn't get the wallpaper scraped off, does it?"

"Why are you so worried about the wallpaper all of a sudden? It's been there for years. Another week won't hurt."

"Oh, yes. I remember now. You said you'd waited for this deal to come through for a long time, so another few months was no big problem. I suppose that goes for the wallpaper, too."

He looked at her for a long moment, his eyebrows drawn together, and then said quietly, "I'm pacing myself. My hands aren't quite back to normal even yet—I still have a little numbness in my fingers. You wouldn't want me to add a good case of carpal tunnel syndrome to my problems, would you?"

Yes, she thought. *In fact, part of me wishes that I'd broken every bone in your hands with that window.*

She didn't look at him. "I thought you were anxious to work on the house, that's all. I'm surprised, if you're not enjoying it as much as you expected, that you'd want to buy more property. What are you trying to do, anyway, own the neighborhood? Settle down in your own little estate?" There was a sharp edge to her voice.

He looked up with a scowl. "Where did you hear about that?"

Then it was true. And if that much was fact, it was all true. Clancey's fists clenched at her sides—out of sight, she hoped. It was the only way she knew to keep her whole body from trembling.

"What difference does it make where I heard it?" The sarcasm had died out of her voice. She shook her head slowly, sadly. "It was unfair, it was cruel, it was stupid—not to tell me the truth, Rowan." The words were almost gentle.

His eyes dropped to the box of brightly colored lights in his hands, and she watched as a dull red flush crept high into his cheeks.

A cold prickle of fear raced through her before she realized it wasn't anger that had made him turn red. There was no fury in his eyes and no threat in the set of his jaw. Instead, Clancey realized with compassion, the color in his face was embarrassment. It might even be humiliation. And if he felt ashamed of what he was doing . . .

"There's still time to clear yourself," she said softly. "I suppose it's too late to convince the city to change the site, but even if the house can't be saved—"

He shook his head abruptly as if trying to clear his ears. "What the hell are you talking about?"

"The civic center." Surely he wasn't going to pretend he didn't understand! "If you didn't actually make money from the deal, then it would be all right, wouldn't it? I mean, it's profiteering that's illegal, not an honest sale, even if you did use your inside knowledge to get the house in the first place."

He didn't answer.

She was suddenly angry again. "Look, I'm only trying to help you out of a tight spot, Rowan. And I know what I'm talking about. Hank told me about your little scheme to collect a share of the taxpayers' money. If the city is going to buy land for the civic center, then you might as well get a handsome settlement—that was it, wasn't it? Don't bother to deny it."

"I'm not going to bother to deny anything." He began to gather up the scrapers and the boxes of lights. The very precision of his movements as he put things back in the paper bag was almost frightening.

He was admitting it, then. There was no remorse in his voice now, and no doubt—only a hard edge that sounded almost hateful.

Still, for just a moment there he had seemed sorry, as if he would welcome a way out. She had to try again.

"Won't you at least talk about it?" she said as gently as she could. "I'm sure we can still find a way for you to make things right, Rowan. If you want to, that is."

He didn't even look at her. "No, thanks, Lady Bountiful. If your idea of helping is to rescue me from my criminal tendencies, I can do without your interference."

"Rowan!"

He picked up the bag and turned toward the front door. "I'll expect you to be out by January first."

As the cold air swirled around her, Clancey sagged onto the stool by the cash register and put her head down into her hands.

This time she hurt too much even to cry.

CHAPTER ELEVEN

DESPITE IT ALL, she wanted to run after him and beg him to come back. And even though Clancey knew her only possible option was to keep her distance from him, it was the weakness in her knees that kept her perched on that high stool, and not the strength of her convictions. Deep inside, she knew that no matter what he might have done, or intended to do, she still wanted him. She still loved him.

You love the man you thought he was, she told herself. *But that's not who he turned out to be, at all.*

She sat there behind the cash register and fought a battle with herself, and it was well past closing time when she finally raised her head. She had no choice right now, she painfully concluded. She couldn't run away, for she had nowhere to go. But she could devote every spare hour to finding a new place for the store, so that the moment the Christmas season finished she'd never have to cross Rowan McKenna's path again.

The decision didn't soothe the raw and aching corners of her heart, but she knew it was the only way. Things would get better eventually—if she could just survive the next few weeks.

The scattered patches of snow melted over the weekend, and the world took on the gloomy gray cast of winter, spiced only by the almost frantic approach of Christmas. The days grew shorter—and yet every hour hung long on Clancey's hands. She hadn't realized before how often she looked at the clock to see if Rowan was free to leave his office yet. Now that she knew how ingrained a habit it had become, she was glad he was staying away.

And perhaps, she reflected drearily, if she kept repeating that to herself often enough she would eventually learn to mean it.

CLANCEY CALLED KAYE McKenna a couple of days before Thanksgiving to tell her she couldn't come for the holiday, after all. She didn't say, though it was certainly the truth, that she would rather be tied to a stake and burned than have to sit across a table from Rowan and give thanks when she felt no gratitude at all, only heartache and resentment and anger. Instead she explained that she'd found a new location for Small World and would be spending the holiday there, getting ready for her move.

Kaye made no more than a polite protest. Clancey thought, *So much for the threat to send a kidnapping force if I didn't show up.* Rowan might have given Kaye any story at all. And even if he'd told the truth—well, political disagreements could run deep, but family pulled together nevertheless, and on this issue Clancey was most definitely the outsider.

So as she painted the walls of her new store, she tried not to think of what the McKenna family might be doing. Were they watching the elaborate parades on television, or were they the sort to be playing basketball in the driveway instead?

She sat down to munch a sandwich at noon and thought of Kaye's big turkey. She started talking to herself just to hear another voice, and before she knew it she was imagining the family banter over dinner and wondering if Rowan's mother was really as dreamy and absentminded as he had pictured her. If only there wasn't this issue standing between them, Clancey might have had a chance to find out....

She found herself asking if it was such a terrible thing he was doing, after all. It was only a house—an old, half-decrepit, long-abused house. Tearing down a house wasn't a crime. There could be a legitimate difference of opinion on whether any given house should be demolished or restored, and though in Clancey's eyes it would be a waste to destroy this particular one, it wouldn't change the course of the world.

"But the issue involves a whole lot more than just the house," she reminded herself. "It's a question of Rowan's ethics." And if solitude and paint fumes were making her begin to question her own judgment on that matter, it was time to quit work.

She put the lid back on the paint can and cleaned up her mess. On her way home she stopped at the convenience store to rent an old movie, in the hope of boring herself to sleep.

And when she saw the headline and the artist's rendering of the new civic center in delicate color on the front page of the local newspaper, she bought a copy. "A souvenir," she told herself wryly. "A memento of a place that doesn't deserve to be destroyed."

That was before she glanced at the story and realized that the site chosen for the civic center was on the other side of the retail area, a couple of miles from Pine Street and the historical district.

Her house—or, more accurately, Rowan's house—had escaped destruction, after all.

The relief was overwhelming. Everything would be all right, she thought, now that the house was safe....

"No, it won't," she reminded herself. Rowan had made light of his shady deal, but the fact remained that his actions had been illegal. Using inside knowledge to make a profit, diverting taxpayers' dollars to the benefit of an individual, running up the costs of a public project in order to enrich himself—those things could have sent him to prison. The fact that his scheme had ultimately been unsuccessful was no credit to Rowan.

No, his actions were things she couldn't forgive, things she couldn't overlook. A man who couldn't be trusted in matters of business couldn't be relied on in other ways, either.

It was over. Clancey's only choice was to pick up the pieces of her life and go on.

BUT SHE'D FORGOTTEN something, after all. There was one more thing she had to do, and one more time she would have to see him. She still owed him another month's rent.

Rowan had said originally that he would come around to collect on the first day of each month. In December that fell on Saturday, and so all day she expected him, bracing herself each time the door opened. When he hadn't come by closing time she found herself confused—half annoyed at him for prolonging the agony, and half puzzled. Even if he didn't particularly want to see her, he'd want to have his money. And now that he didn't have a windfall from the city government to look forward to...

Then it occurred to her that Kaye would surely have told him about the new storefront. He might be expecting her to move at once, despite the interruption to her Christmas business, in order to avoid paying rent on two places.

Was he expecting to come by later and find the house cleaned out and empty? That wouldn't be a pleasant scene for either of them.

The longer Clancey thought about it, the less she liked the possibility. It might be days before he stopped in to check his property, and the mere idea of sitting there and waiting for him to turn up was enough to make her nerves crawl like cobras.

"When there's something you don't like to do," she reminded herself, "face it fast and get it over with. It hurts less that way."

So she wrote out her check with a hand that shook slightly, making her signature appear rather odd, and looked up his address in the telephone book. Then, before she could talk herself out of it, she drove across town to the high-rise condominium complex where he lived.

The address would have surprised her if she had chanced to look it up before. People who lived in that tower didn't generally consider taking on an old, half-decrepit house in a problematic neighborhood. Hank was right; buying the house made no sense at all for someone like Rowan McKenna.

"It's just too bad I didn't check it out earlier," Clancey muttered as the silent elevator zoomed up a dozen stories. "I might have started asking questions sooner, and saved myself a whole lot of pain."

But her ordeal was almost over now, she told herself bracingly. All she had to do was ring the bell, hand him the rent, make sure he understood that she wouldn't be out till the end of the month, and run for her life. . . . A simple plan, easy to follow.

Except that when she pressed the bell, she didn't hear footsteps coming to answer it. Instead, a far-off voice called, "Come in!"

He must be expecting company, then. And just as obviously, it wasn't Clancey for whom he was waiting.

She drew a long, deep breath and debated whether she should just stand there and ring again in a little while. But her courage was giving out. She wasn't certain it would last even another minute, so she pushed the door open and almost tiptoed in.

The foyer was small, and her shoes tapped noisily against the ceramic tile on the floor. She bit her lip and looked around, into the living room, down a short hallway. There was no one to be seen.

Rowan's head, with a telephone pressed to his ear, appeared around the corner of a door at the far end of the hall, and even at that distance Clancey could see the expression that flared in his eyes. It wasn't the familiar green glow of mischief, but something she'd never seen before.

And it was something she hoped never to see again; it made her nervous. She put her hand to her mouth, hoping to make her lower lip stop trembling, and tried to concentrate on the apartment itself. It was very sleek and contemporary—ivory carpets and drapes, overstuffed furniture, stylish little tables. There was only one thing that would have fit nicely into the house on Pine Street—a glass-and-mahogany cabinet that displayed at least a hundred paperweights of all sizes, shapes and colors. She moved to the doorway of the living room to get a better look.

There was certainly no sign that he intended to close the apartment up anytime soon. There wasn't an item out of place. The surface of the smoked-glass dining table held only a basket of silk flowers.

But then, she'd hardly expected to see boxes, tape, marking pens and tissue paper, had she?

She didn't hear him coming until he was directly behind her, and when he spoke she jumped almost a foot.

"What have I done to earn this honor, Clancey?"

His tone was faintly ironic, and it stung like salt rubbed into a fresh cut.

She took the slightly crumpled check from her coat pocket and held it out to him. "I wanted to deliver this personally so you can't say I was late with the rent," she said stiffly.

A muscle at the corner of his mouth twitched a little. He inspected the check with insulting care.

Clancey hadn't planned to turn this visit into an attack, but she was unable to stop herself. "It's too bad if you expected me to move right now, but a deal is a deal, right?"

Rowan folded the check and slipped it into his money clip. He still didn't say anything.

The silence goaded Clancey past endurance. "Don't worry, I'll be out before the first of the year, as we agreed."

"Are you happy with your new place?" His voice was softer than she'd expected it to be; it sounded sincere.

Perhaps it was genuine, she thought, with a tinge of regret for her own sharpness. Whatever other plans he had nurtured, he'd never seemed to want to force her out of business.

She shrugged. The gesture looked casual, but it hurt; her whole body was tensed, and she felt as if the muscles in her shoulders were tearing as she moved. "It will do."

"I shouldn't have said what I did—telling you to get out."

"Why not? Obviously you meant it. What are you going to do with the house, anyway?"

"I haven't decided. You don't have to move at all, you know. Not right away, at least."

"I know," Clancey said crisply. "I read the newspapers. But—well, let's just say I'll be glad to leave. Perhaps I'll sell out completely, and try my luck somewhere else." Some other town, she thought, where she wouldn't be tempted to look for him on every street corner, in every car that passed by. "It's probably time to move on."

He stared down at her for a single moment that seemed to stretch into eternity. "Tell me, Clancey, what did I ever do to make you hate me so much?"

She couldn't react quickly enough to keep the stricken look out of her face, or stop herself from looking up at him.

"And yet, you don't hate this," he whispered.

His mouth came down on hers, hard and hungry and demanding. There was not even a hint of gentleness about him then, but despite the fierceness of his embrace, it took every ounce of Clancey's strength to keep herself from kissing him back with all the fire that he roused in her, to keep from giving him all the response he could desire.

When finally he raised his head, she said with the last of her breath, "Do you really think that proves anything, Rowan?"

He put her aside, almost roughly, and she stooped to retrieve her keys, which had dropped unheeded to the floor in the midst of that…assault, she supposed, was the only accurate word for it.

"Maybe I'll just demolish the damned house," he said. His hands were outspread, fingers rigid, as if he was longing to rip boards one from another by brute force. "There would be great satisfaction in tearing it apart piece by piece."

"You don't expect that threat to bother me anymore, do you? That's why you bought it, after all—to destroy it. Just my bad luck I got in your way, wasn't it?"

Rowan's jaw tightened. "Your bad luck? Maybe. It was certainly mine."

The tone of his voice stung. Clancey clenched her fists till her nails dug into her palms. "You certainly can't blame me for all of it. It wasn't my plan to bulldoze it."

"And not mine, either. I intend—I intended to live in that house."

"Oh, sure," she mocked. "Glass-and-steel furniture and all. Who's going to prove what you might have intended? But I'm not stupid, Rowan, so don't bother to lie to me."

"I'm damn tired of having my word questioned, Clancey."

There was something about the icy blue glitter in his eyes that made her take a step back. But she couldn't stop herself from saying, "Just because you misjudged the council, or didn't have quite as much political pull as you thought you had—"

"Oh, I've got pull, all right, don't worry about that." He sounded almost grim. "I know all the right people, and exactly how to make them move."

"But—"

He walked across the living room and stared out at the city's skyline. "If you've finished, Clancey... Thank you for delivering the check."

She didn't stir. Pieces were clicking together in her mind. "You fixed it," she said. "You knew they were going to choose that site, and you thought better of the whole thing and fixed it so they picked the other one instead."

Rowan winced. "No, I didn't, dammit."

"But then—"

"I can show you the list of sites the council considered. Pine Street wasn't on it."

"But you admitted the whole thing!" She almost choked on the words.

"I didn't admit anything."

Clancey shook her head vehemently. "You as much as said—"

"*You* said a lot of things that night. I—" He paused and then added heavily, "I just didn't think it was worth defending myself."

He was right, she realized. He'd said almost nothing. She'd thought it was simply because he was annoyed at being caught out. "If it wasn't true, why would you have let me believe all that?" she whispered.

"You didn't exactly give me the benefit of the doubt, Clancey."

Her head drooped guiltily. "It was so obvious—"

"To Hank, maybe it was. You might find it handy to remember that Hank is usually about six weeks slow with his facts."

"And exactly what does that mean?"

Rowan's eyebrows raised at the challenge in her voice. "That he wasn't completely mistaken, just behind the times. Pine Street was on an early list of possible sites. A list I stumbled across when I was finishing up all the paperwork to get the house. As it turns out, it was eliminated as soon as the historical people started making noise.''

''People like Kaye?''

''Yes,'' he said dryly. ''And just how do you think Kaye found out, anyway? Who do you think tipped her off to mobilize her troops?''

Was that what he had meant about knowing the right people? Clancey's throat had almost closed up. ''But the petitions and everything—she was working on it till the announcement was made. For all I know she's still at it. If it was eliminated weeks ago—''

''She's trying to prevent problems from sneaking up on them in the future, the way this one did.''

If the historical district was enlarged, Clancey thought, the safeguards would be automatic. And if all this was true, then Rowan should get a great deal of credit for it.

He turned, staring out across the city again, and added softly, ''But you took Hank's word for everything, didn't you? You didn't even ask me.''

She jammed her hands into the pockets of her jacket, nails biting into her palms. ''Of course I asked you,'' she said, almost under her breath. ''You admitted you were buying other houses on the block, too.'' She crossed over to the window. ''What about that, Rowan? Why did you want those other houses, if you weren't planning to hold up the city for a nice profit?''

He shook his head a little. ''I was only trying to buy the ones on each side, for protection, and I was trying to keep it quiet so the prices didn't skyrocket. It's not the world's best neighborhood at the moment, you know. Owning a little extra green space seemed like a good idea." He didn't look at her. "At least, it did when I still wanted to live there. Now... Well, I wish they would blast the damned house down with dynamite. It would save me a good deal of trouble."

There was a sour, bitter taste in Clancey's mouth. Her reasoning had been so perfectly clear, so perfectly damning and so perfectly wrong. And now even the attempt to explain how she'd reached such an insane, stupid conclusion would be useless.

I should have known, she thought. *I should have trusted him, no matter what.*

But it was too late for that. There could be no patching things up anymore, for having broken their growing trust, she'd then ground the pieces under her heel until nothing remained. If it hadn't been worth it to him even to defend himself...

Rowan straightened his shoulders and turned slightly. "Now that we've got it all straightened out—"

"But we haven't." Clancey stared blindly out the window, trying to figure out how and where she'd gone so wrong. "If you weren't turning red from guilt that night, then what was it? Anger? Or embarrassment, maybe? What on earth—"

"Clancey, please don't."

Her head drooped. "I know. You want me to get out of your sight. I'm going. I just want you to know that I'm sorry, Rowan. I'm so very sorry."

She turned toward the door, and it was then she saw the bear—the panda bear with the sad, far-seeing eyes that Rowan had bought at Small World weeks ago. He was sitting sternly upright in the corner of an overstuffed chair. Clancey cautiously picked him up. The furry little body warmed quickly to her touch.

"Clancey—" Rowan said, and took a step toward her.

At the same instant she held out the bear. "You didn't buy him as an ornament for this room, surely. You couldn't have. He doesn't fit the decor."

"No." He sounded hoarse. "Clancey—"

"Then why is he here? You said it was a peacekeeping mission, but—"

"Damn the bear, Clancey." Then he sighed and rubbed the heel of his hand across his forehead as if his head hurt. "I bought it for Kaye, if you must know. She collects the silly things, and I was going to take it to her when I told her about the civic center."

"But you kept him instead." Clancey wet her lips with the tip of her tongue. "Rowan, why did you keep the bear?"

He stopped and scowled at her. "Oh, what difference does it make? Because it reminded me of you, that's why. Those big sad eyes..."

She was afraid to hope, and yet—surely there was something left between them, something to build on. If both of them wanted to build...

"Dammit, Clancey, don't look at me as if you're hungry!"

"Even if I am?" She moved just a little closer to him, carefully, as if he were a wild animal who might dart away at any moment. "Rowan, can you ever forgive me for what I've done?"

For an endless moment she was afraid that he was going to ignore her plea. Finally he said heavily, "I don't know. It depends."

She took another cautious step. "On what?"

He didn't look at her. "On why you turned away from me. Why you couldn't trust me. Why you as-

sumed I was guilty, and didn't even ask me straight out
for the truth.''

She could hear the sound of her own blood hammering loudly in her ears, and knew that this was the
only chance she'd be given. She closed her eyes and
looked deep into her heart, and then she said, ''Because as long as I didn't ask, even though I suspected
the worst, I could still preserve my own picture of
you—my idealistic image of what I thought you were.
I didn't want to have my doubts confirmed. What I
believed I'd discovered was a terrible thing, but it
would have been even worse if you had belittled my
dream of you, or said straight out that you weren't who
I had thought you were.'' She swallowed hard. It might
do no good whatever, but there was no other option
now but sacrificing every gram of her pride. ''The man
I loved,'' she finished steadily.

He looked at her without expression, as if he hadn't
heard what she'd said—or as if it didn't matter. ''Not
because you hated me?'' he said woodenly.

She was so light-hearted from holding her breath
that she was swaying. ''I could never hate you,
Rowan.''

He said, almost casually, ''I was going to ask you to
marry me, if you'd gone to dinner with me that night.''

Clancey sucked in a deep breath, and the oxygen hit
her with a rush. *But that was then,* she reminded herself. *This is now. Things have changed.* ''Thank you
for that,'' she whispered.

''But when I came back with the Christmas lights,
you'd changed somehow, and I didn't have any clue
why. I thought at first it was because you suspected I
was in love with you, and you wanted to discourage me
before I embarrassed myself by proposing.''

Clancey was breathing as if she'd just finished a race.

"Then you started in with accusations about my criminal tendencies. And I knew if you could believe that of me..."

She shook her head. "Don't you see?" she whispered. "I was afraid. It was breaking my heart to think you were dishonest, yet I still wanted you so much."

When his arms came around her once more, hard and strong and comforting, she buried her face in his shoulder and sobbed in the way that a terrified child cried—after the danger was over, when it was safe to let go and wail.

He held her close and caught her tears with his fingertips and murmured soothing words into her ear—words that were so intriguing she soon lost interest in crying.

He gently pulled her down onto the deep couch beside him and kissed her. And it was a long time later that he said, "Now we can get down to plans. How much of what you said you'd do with the house was serious? I was never quite sure."

She blew her nose and settled back against him with a sigh. "Most of it."

"Then we'll do it."

"You just said you wanted to dynamite the place."

"Not if I can share it with you."

"Oh," she said softly. "Is that why you weren't making any progress with the wallpaper—because you weren't sure about me?"

Rowan pulled slightly away and looked down at her incredulously. "What do you mean, no progress? There are seven layers of that stuff under the paint, and it was put on with industrial-strength glue."

She smiled a little. "And the boxes of toys you were exploring? What about them?"

He had the grace to look a trifle ashamed of himself.

Clancey relented. "It was very considerate of you to wait and let me have a say in the decorating scheme." She glanced around the apartment. "Not that this is bad, exactly, but—"

He sighed. "I know. It's got no personality. It was a reaction to living amidst old stuff all my life, you see. I'm the middle child, and it seemed to me that I had hand-me-down everything. I wanted a new look, so when I was dating an interior decorator a couple of years ago—"

She snapped her fingers. "That explains the silk flowers."

"Yes. Well, I've always liked Kaye's house, and I was ready for a change. I just didn't know how big a change I was getting."

"That's a safe statement."

"Besides, there you were, keeping everything stirred up. I thought I was coming around to check on the house, but from the first night—no, the second one, perhaps—I ought to have known it was you I was coming to see."

"And I thought you didn't care," she said, so softly that he had to bend his head to hear. "I practically begged you to make love to me, and when you didn't—"

"Things were moving too fast. The night the ceiling fell, I knew how important you were becoming to me. But I'm sort of old-fashioned that way. I wanted us to be friends first, and lovers last. And I was afraid that if I let myself go and really kissed you, I might not be able to stop at that. So..."

She thought it over and smiled. "I would have understood," she murmured. "Whenever things really get out of hand, it's just the mushroom factor at work."

"Well, we've certainly got a first-class case of it. Now Small World has two locations. What are you going to do about that?"

Clancey shrugged. "It was nice in theory, but living above the store wasn't working out very well."

"I was hoping you'd say that. We'll need the room someday, for our kids."

"Our kids?"

"It would be a shame if all those toys of yours were never played with again, don't you think? Marry me, Clancey?"

She frowned and chewed thoughtfully on her index fingernail, and then shook her head. "Can't. I promised a long time ago to make no legal claim on you or your house. Ever."

Rowan growled like a grizzly bear and pushed her down on to the couch.

She shrieked and tried to fend him off, but it would have been impossible to push him away, even if her heart had really been in it. So finally—but only after he had kissed her quite unmercifully—Clancey yielded, and gracefully agreed to take her chances as his wife.

After all, she told herself, she certainly owed him the benefit of the doubt.

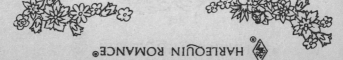

HARLEQUIN ROMANCE®

Some people have the spirit
of Christmas all year round...

People like Blake Connors
and Karin Palmer.

Meet them—and love them!—in
Eva Rutland's
ALWAYS CHRISTMAS.

Harlequin Romance #3240
Available in December wherever
Harlequin books are sold.

HRHX

HARLEQUIN ✦ PRESENTS ®

BARBARY WHARF

Home to the *Sentinel*
Home to passion, heartache and love

Charlotte Lamb

The BARBARY WHARF six-book saga continues with
Book Three, TOO CLOSE FOR COMFORT. Esteban
Sebastian is the *Sentinel*'s marketing director *and* the
company heartthrob. But beautiful Irena Olivero wants
nothing to do with him—he's always too close for comfort.

And don't forget media tycoon Nick Caspian and his
adversary Gina Tyrrell. Their never-ending arguments are
legendary—but is it possible that things are not quite what
they seem?

TOO CLOSE FOR COMFORT (Harlequin Presents
#1513) available in December.

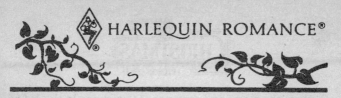

HARLEQUIN ROMANCE®

After her father's heart attack, Stephanie Bloomfield comes home to Orchard Valley, Oregon, to be with him and with her sisters.

Orchard Valley

Steffie learns that many things have changed in her absence—but not her feelings for journalist Charles Tomaselli. He was the reason she left Orchard Valley. Now, three years later, will he give her a reason to stay?

"The Orchard Valley trilogy features three delightful, spirited sisters and a trio of equally fascinating men. The stories are rich with the romance, warmth of heart and humor readers expect, and invariably receive, from Debbie Macomber."

—Linda Lael Miller

Don't miss the Orchard Valley trilogy by Debbie Macomber:

VALERIE   Harlequin Romance #3232 (November 1992)
STEPHANIE   Harlequin Romance #3239 (December 1992)
NORAH   Harlequin Romance #3244 (January 1993)

Look for the special cover flash on each book!

Available wherever Harlequin books are sold.   ORC-2

·HARLEQUIN·
·HISTORICAL·

CHRISTMAS

·STORIES·1992·

Capture the magic and romance of Christmas in the 1800s with **HARLEQUIN HISTORICAL CHRISTMAS STORIES 1992**, a collection of three stories by celebrated historical authors. The perfect Christmas gift!

Don't miss these heartwarming stories, available in November wherever Harlequin books are sold:

MISS MONTRACHET REQUESTS by Maura Seger
CHRISTMAS BOUNTY by Erin Yorke
A PROMISE KEPT by Bronwyn Williams

Plus, as an added bonus, you can receive a FREE keepsake Christmas ornament. Just collect four proofs of purchase from any November or December 1992 Harlequin or Silhouette series novels, or from any Harlequin or Silhouette Christmas collection, and receive a beautiful dated brass Christmas candle ornament.

Mail this certificate along with four (4) proof-of-purchase coupons plus $1.50 postage and handling (check or money order—do not send cash), payable to Harlequin Books, to: **In the U.S.:** P.O. Box 9057, Buffalo, NY 14269-9057; **In Canada:** P.O. Box 622, Fort Erie, Ontario, L2A 5X3.

ONE PROOF OF PURCHASE

Name: _____

_____

Address: _____

_____

City: _____

State/Province: _____

Zip/Postal Code: _____

HX92POP   093 KAG